## She tried a different approach

After all, she'd had to fend men off before. "If you carry on like that, Pasquale," she said reasonably, "then you'll really leave me no choice other than to scream, and I'm sure that would do your reputation no good whatsoever."

"My reputation is of no concern to me," he drawled with dismissive arrogance. "But if that is what you intend to do, then I must give you fair warning that you will really leave *me* no choice other than to silence you most satisfactorily."

Her confusion must have shown in her eyes. "By kissing you, of course," he elaborated silkily. "And as I recall you liked me kissing you, didn't you, Suki? You liked it *ve-ry* much!"

**SHARON KENDRICK** was born in west London, England, and has had *heaps* of jobs, which have included photography, nursing, driving an ambulance across the Australian desert and cooking her way around Europe in a converted double-decker bus! Without a doubt, writing is the best job she has ever had, and when she's not dreaming up new heroes (some of which are based on her doctor husband) she likes cooking, reading, drinking wine, listening to West Coast music and talking to her two children, Celia and Patrick.

## Books by Sharon Kendrick

HARLEQUIN PRESENTS
1820—PART-TIME FATHER

# SHARON KENDRICK

## Mistress Material

**Harlequin Books**

TORONTO • NEW YORK • LONDON
AMSTERDAM • PARIS • SYDNEY • HAMBURG
STOCKHOLM • ATHENS • TOKYO • MILAN
MADRID • WARSAW • BUDAPEST • AUCKLAND

ISBN 0-373-11867-8

MISTRESS MATERIAL

First North American Publication 1997.

Copyright © 1996 by Sharon Kendrick.

This edition published by arrangement with Harlequin Books S.A.

® and TM are trademarks of the publisher. Trademarks indicated with ® are registered in the United States Patent and Trademark Office, the Canadian Trade Marks Office and in other countries.

Printed in U.S.A.

# CHAPTER ONE

IT COULDN'T be! Suki thought frantically. Not him! Anyone but him! And yet who else could it be? For who on earth could be mistaken for Pasquale Caliandro—the most diabolical man it had ever been her misfortune to meet?

Dear God, please no, she prayed silently, but she could do absolutely nothing to stop the slow pull of desire unfurling in the pit of her stomach as her traitorous eyes feasted themselves on the most delectable example of the male species she had ever seen in twenty-four years.

And she had seen the lot.

In the course of her career she had worked with male models, actors and rock stars—whose seductive faces and sexy bodies graced the bedroom walls of millions of women all over the world. But not one, not a single one, had come even close to the kind of impact that this man had on her. And not just her, either, she observed caustically, since every other woman present seemed hypnotised by that spectacular, long-legged frame.

Suki's heart was thumping erratically. What the hell was he doing *here*, in the South of France? And what on earth should she do? She wondered if he'd seen her—but even if he had, would he remember the brazen young girl who had offered her body so eagerly to him when she was barely seventeen?

Completely forgetting that she'd loosened the thin gold straps of her bikini, Suki struggled to sit up, but she couldn't tear her eyes away from him, and then she saw that he was moving. He was walking.

*Towards her!*

She gave a helpless little whimper as her eyes were drawn to the powerful thrust of his thighs. Then upwards. Dear Lord! This man didn't need to flaunt himself in tight jeans—indeed, she suspected that if he ventured outside in anything other than the cool, pale, beautifully cut linen trousers he wore he would be arrested immediately for indecent exposure.

Up still further her eyes roamed. Oh, what a chest! A broad, powerful sweep of hair-darkened muscle beneath the cream silk of his shirt.

Her mouth dried as her eyes finally reached his face, lingering all too briefly on the beautifully shaped lips which somehow managed to be both sensual and cruel. And that nose—with its proud, aristocratic Roman curve. Who would have guessed that a nose could be such a turn-on? she thought, unable to stop herself from ogling it, like an art-lover confronted with a masterpiece for the first time ever. Reluctantly, her gaze drifted upwards to meet his eyes, and her heart stilled as she acknowledged the cold fire and the contempt which sparked from the dark depths and which he made no effort whatsoever to hide.

His mouth was nothing more than a derisory slash as he reached her lounger and towered over her. 'So,' he drawled contemptuously, 'I see that the years have done little to temper your appetites, *cara*.'

Her precariously thin veneer of sophistication was vanquished in a moment by the wounding words, delivered in the deepest, sexiest voice she had ever heard, an intriguing mixture of transatlantic with a seductive European undertone.

Logical thought was impossible, and she was instantly on the defensive. 'And what's that supposed to mean?' she demanded furiously.

'Oh, come *on*...' The mouth twisted with devilish scorn. 'I refer to your leisurely scrutiny of my body, Suzanna.'

'Suki,' she corrected immediately.

Dark eyebrows were raised in a silent and aloof query. 'Ah! Of course—*Suki*.' He emphasised the word so that it sounded like some sultry profanity. 'The name you acquired along with your glittering fame as a model, and your many lovers...'

Her mouth fell open and she made a little murmur of protest at such a patent untruth, but he carried on regardless. 'But no matter,' he said softly as he surveyed her from slitted, dangerous eyes, 'what you call yourself. Your basic gutter instincts remain the same, do they not? You looked as if you would like to eat me up. Every *inch* of me,' he emphasised hatefully.

Swine!

Colour rushed up to form two heated flares over her high cheekbones as she tossed the thick waves of her hair back over her slender shoulders. Head held high, she spoke from a throat which felt as if it had been lined with the roughest, coarsest sandpaper. 'You flatter yourself, Pasquale!' she shot back. 'But then you always did!'

He gave a small smile then, allowed it to linger and play around his lips. 'Do I—*Suki*?' he returned silkily. 'Flatter myself?' And the sudden change in the timbre of his voice, the velvet caress as he spoke her name, sent her senses jangling. The flow of blood around her veins altered; became slow and heavy. She felt the pulse-points beating insistently at her temples, her wrists...and...shamefully...deep, deep within her groin as he stared down at her.

But more was to follow as his eyes roamed almost indifferently over her face, seemingly careless of her enormous eyes gazing helplessly at him or of her wide mouth throbbing in an unconsciously provocative *moue*.

The only flash of life and of interest came when his gaze came at last to alight on her breasts and then the indifference was replaced by a feral light and his eyes darkened as they took in the lush, creamy mounds. She felt them tingle, become heavy and swollen, the tips burning with tingling excitement. And as he gave a coldly triumphant smile she realised to her horror that the forgotten bikini-top had slipped right down, exposing most of her for his scathing delectation. 'Oh, no!' she cried, and clapped both palms protectively over her breasts.

He said something very softly in Italian as his eyes narrowed. 'Please do not cover them, *cara*,' he murmured, on a husky entreaty. 'Such magnificent breasts. How I long to touch them. To take each tip into my mouth and to suckle each one until—'

Suki grabbed a towel and threw it over herself, squirming with embarrassment and an excitement which was painfully acute as she struggled to haul the flimsy gold material back into place, but faced with that look of hunger in those dark, magnificent eyes she was all fingers and thumbs.

She hadn't seen him for seven years, and yet two minutes in his company was enough to plunge her into dark and erotic waters which were threatening to completely submerge her. It was a nightmare. 'Get—away from me,' she managed, on a croak. *'Now!'*

He didn't move; he didn't need to—because he was actually standing beside her, not touching her at all, but at her words he seemed to pull himself together, because the raw heat of need was wiped from his face leaving nothing but a coldly contemptuous mask. 'Certainly,' he concurred, in a voice which was strangely harsh and a touch unsteady. 'There is little pleasure to be gained from a woman who offers herself so freely.'

Stung, Suki glared up at him from narrow amber eyes which threatened to glimmer with tears of self-disgust. But she kept them at bay.

Just.

'I wouldn't offer myself to you if you were the last man in the universe!'

'No? You have undergone a radical change of personality, then?' he mocked.

What could she say? She wasn't hypocritical enough to deny just how dreadfully she had once behaved with Pasquale Caliandro.

Still clutching the towel to her, she sat up, and the glint in his eye was unmistakable. Curiosity warred with common sense, and curiosity won hands down. 'What are you doing here?' she demanded, her heart beginning to race erratically as a schoolgirlish hope she'd thought long dead re-emerged with startling strength. 'You haven't—followed me here?'

To her fury, he actually threw his dark head back and laughed aloud, a glorious, mellifluous sound which made several people turn round to look at them. But when he'd stopped laughing the face which regarded her was cold and unsmiling. 'Followed you?' he queried, and the trace of sardonic incredulity made her blood boil. 'Now why on earth should I want to do that?'

Suki shrugged, a desire for revenge chipping away at her insistently. 'Your reputation with women is legendary,' she said coolly.

'Is it, now?' he queried softly. 'I wasn't aware that you had such *intimate* knowledge of my behaviour.'

She sought to disillusion him of the idea that she somehow spent all her spare time finding out about him and his fabled exploits with the fairer sex. 'I read the gossip columns like everyone else,' she said.

'Ah!' He nodded. 'So you do. But at least, *cara*, I do not have the reputation of breaking up other people's relationships. Unlike you,' he accused, and he nodded again when he saw her colour heighten. 'Yes,' he affirmed. 'You see, I too read the gossip columns.'

Oh, those *wretched* tabloids! According to them, she'd had more lovers than Mata Hari! 'If you're referring to that ridiculous scandal in New York—that was a pack of lies!' Suki defended hotly.

He raised a disbelieving eyebrow. 'Oh, really? So the photographer's girlfriend made the whole thing up, did she? You *weren't* sleeping with her boyfriend?'

'No, I *wasn't*!'

His mouth curved contemptuously. 'And the newly married Arabian prince who courted you so assiduously in front of his young bride last year... Tell me, was that also a pack of lies?'

Suki sighed as she remembered *that* sorry little affair. She'd met Prince Abdul at a cocktail party thrown by the Foreign Office in Paris. He had been ridiculously infatuated—mostly, Suki suspected, because she hadn't been the slightest bit interested in him. He had always had everything he'd always wanted, and he had wanted *her*!

He had actually asked her to be his second bride—but without even bothering to divorce the first one! She had intended telling Prince Abdul exactly what she thought of him, but one of the diplomats at the Foreign Office had sought her out for a quiet word. There was a big oil deal going through between Prince Abdul's country and Britain. Best not to actually turn him down outright, but to let him down gently...

In fact, afterwards the diplomat had told her that she had been a great help to her country— maybe Pasquale should hear about *that*! She held her head up proudly and looked him straight in the eye. 'There happens to be a perfectly simple explanation for that,' she said reasonably.

But it seemed that he wasn't interested in reason, or an explanation, because his dark eyes were boring into hers, an expression of scorn lifting the corner of his exquisite mouth. 'And even given *my* supposed reputation,' he gritted, 'do you somehow imagine that I am so desperate as to follow and to find you? You who are everything that I most despise in a woman?'

Stung by the biting criticism, Suki was momentarily lost for words, her cheeks flaring at the denigrating accusation he'd thrown at her. Yes, OK, she hadn't behaved too well, but surely her foolish youthful behaviour with him didn't warrant *that* kind of censure? 'I really don't think that's fair...' she faltered.

But he had crouched down so that their eyes were on a level, and she could almost see the hostility emanating from him in pure waves towards her. 'When I go searching for a woman,' he said deliberately, 'it will be for someone as unlike you as possible. Though I'm not sure that she exists— because I've certainly never come across her.

'You see, Suki, I'm waiting for the woman who doesn't give me the green light the instant that I meet her. Most men—and certainly this man—are turned on by the thrill of the chase before the capture. Something which is gained so easily has little intrinsic value, I believe.'

Suki was shaken to the core by the depth of his dislike, but she was damned sure she wouldn't show it. Her amber eyes glinted dangerously. 'I don't have to lie here and listen to this—'

'No, indeed,' he agreed, in his deep drawl, his eyes hot and hungry with sexual mischief. 'I have a much better idea. Why don't we move away? You could lie down somewhere else. With me...'

Somehow he managed to imbue the suggestion with so much sensual promise that it took Suki every last ounce of pride she possessed to answer him back. 'Spare me your cheap innuendo!' she said, her eyes sparking amber fire. 'And make your mind up! Either you despise me so much that my very presence contaminates you or you're extending an extremely unsubtle invitation to get me into bed with you—you can't do both, Pasquale.' She shook her head sadly. 'Dear, dear—a supposedly intelligent man like you really ought to be able to see such gaping holes in your logic.'

She saw the warning light of battle in his eyes, but when he spoke his voice was very soft. 'A man does not always think with his head,' he said insultingly.

That did it! 'Get out of my way,' she said from between gritted teeth, and she swung her long,

faintly tanned legs over the side of the lounger.
First glancing down to check that she was halfway
decent, she dropped the towel onto the lounger,
then got to her feet, looking around in vain for
Salvatore, the photographer who had brought her
to this house-party outside Cannes.

It was *supposed* to have been the relaxing finale
to two days of solid shooting for a book of
photographs Salvatore was producing. Relaxing—huh! About as relaxing as being on the
front line of a war-zone, with the arrival of
Pasquale Caliandro. Suki began to move away.

'Oh, no. Not so fast.' In a single, snake-like
movement Pasquale had captured her tiny wrist
in the strong grasp of his hand and Suki was hor-
rified how her body thrilled to that first contact
of flesh on flesh. And why did he have to be so
tall? So powerful? So gorgeous? Her throat
constricted.

'Let me go—'

He shook his head with implacable confidence. 'No. You and I need to talk.'

'I have nothing to say to you—'

'But I,' he said, and his voice was husky with
intent, 'have plenty to say to you.'

'I'm not interested.' But oh, what a lie, for despite her instinctive and purely protective need to
put as much distance between them as possible
she was *bursting* to know what he wanted—and
she was certain that he'd guessed as much.

He gave a small, humourless smile. 'On the
contrary—I think you might be.'

He still held her wrist and she was powerless to move, and Suki realised that to an outsider it would appear that he was holding her lightly, almost affectionately—the steely determination of his grip would not be apparent to anyone else.

She tried a different approach. After all, she'd had to fend men off before. She tipped her head to one side, so that the long curls—the colour of golden syrup glinting in the sunshine, or so she'd been told—fell over her bosom. 'If you carry on like that, Pasquale,' she said reasonably, 'then you'll really leave me no choice other than to scream, and I'm sure that would do your reputation no good whatsoever.'

'My reputation is of no concern to me,' he drawled with dismissive arrogance. 'But if that is what you intend to do, then I must give you fair warning that you will really leave *me* no choice other than to silence you most satisfactorily.'

Her confusion must have shown in her eyes. 'By kissing you, of course,' he elaborated silkily. 'And as I recall you liked me kissing you, didn't you, Suki? You liked it *ve-ry* much.'

*Oh!* That occasional lilt to his voice was so devilishly attractive! Suki took a deep breath and met his gaze full-on. 'What do you want?'

'To talk to you.'

'And that's all?'

'For now.' The words sounded ominous.

She'd been little more than a child when she'd known him before, and then she had been so enraptured by his physical magnetism that she had seen little beyond his tantalising exterior. Now, as an adult, she recognised the quiet determination about the man which he wore like a mantle. If Pasquale wanted to talk to her, she realised, then attempting to avoid him might prove to be more trouble than it was worth.

'Very well,' she sighed. 'Talk to me. I'm listening. But I'm giving you five minutes to say whatever it is you want to say—and then I'm out of here!'

'Out—of—here,' he repeated slowly, in a voice of fascinated horror. He made a little clicking sound of disapproval. 'Such an expensive Swiss education,' he mused. 'Wasted. That all those years of tuition should culminate in such bald, inelegant little statements...'

His elegant censure hit a raw nerve as something inside her snapped. The realisation that he was playing with her, teasing her, as an angler would a fish, made Suki realise that she was putting herself into an unnecessarily weak position. She didn't *have* to stay and talk to him. She didn't *have* to do anything. She was no longer a naïve and gullible schoolgirl—she was an independent career-woman in her own right, for heaven's sake!

Without another word, she stalked off towards the house, pushing her way through the milling throng, but she knew from the buzz which accompanied her movements that Pasquale was following her.

Let him follow her! she thought with a stubborn resurgence of resolve. She would slam the wretched door in his face and then lock it! That would call his bluff. He had arrogantly stated that his reputation was of no concern to him, but she doubted whether he would want this select and privileged bunch of guests witnessing him beating her door down!

She was aware of people watching them, of the women staring at Pasquale, their eyes full of ill-concealed lust. She had been like that once. She shuddered in disgust as she glanced over her shoulder to see that he had paused to speak to one of the waitresses. Vaguely, Suki wondered where Salvatore was, but he was nowhere to be seen. But then perhaps it was better that he wasn't around. He would want to know who Pasquale was—and how could she tell him? How could she say, He's the brother of the girl who was my best friend—the man I once begged to make love to me?

And he hadn't.

That was the most galling thing.

He hadn't.

It was a story she was not proud of and to this day it had the power to make her flinch when she remembered exactly how she had behaved. Over the years she had deliberately pushed the memory to the recesses of her mind and seeing him today had brought it all flooding back with painful clarity.

She slipped through the house, her bare feet moving over the cold marble floors, her tall, dark, silent pursuer making her heart thunder with dread and excitement.

Her room was on the first floor, at the opposite end of the corridor to Salvatore's, and she
hurriedly pushed the door open, aware of
Pasquale's footsteps, of the soft sound of his
breath, of that strange, elusive masculine scent,
still so startlingly familiar, even after seven years.

She turned to face him, her chest heaving, her
almond-shaped amber eyes narrowed like a lion-
ess's. 'This is ridiculous,' she said.

His face was infuriatingly enigmatic. 'I agree,'
he returned. 'You are injecting an element of
farce into my simple request that we talk.'

She thought of the intimacy of the room just
behind them. 'Very well,' she said. 'But not here.'

He smiled, but the smile did not reach his cold,
glittering eyes. 'Oh? And why not—or can I
guess? The presence of a bed bothers you, does
it, Suki? Are you afraid of what might happen
if you're alone in a bedroom with me?'

She swallowed. All those nights she'd spent
imagining how she'd behave if she ever had the
misfortune to see him again. She had planned to
ignore him, look down her nose at him. In her
wilder fantasies she had even been prepared to
pretend not to recognise him at all, planning to
stare at that dark, handsome face with bemused
bewilderment, although looking at him now she
knew that that would have been asking a little
*too* much of her general acting ability.

It had certainly not been her intention to let
him know that his presence still had the power
to disturb her. Profoundly. And wasn't that
exactly what she was doing now?

Taking a deep breath, she switched into super-ficial hostess mode. Giving him the bright smile she normally reserved for the lens of a camera, she waved her hand invitingly.

'Forgive me,' she said, sounding deliberately insincere, and saw from the cold twist of his mouth that her insincerity had been noted. 'I've been under a lot of strain recently—working too hard—you know how it is.' She glanced down at the waterproof watch on her wrist and gave him a cool, self-possessed smile. 'I can give you—ten minutes. Is that time enough?'

'Plenty,' he said abrasively, and followed her into the room.

He walked over to the window, where the balcony overlooked the poolside, and there was silence for a moment as he stared down at people tearing apart the glistening red lobsters which the waiters had now produced, at women delicately devouring the sweet pink flesh as they tried not to smear their lipstick. Suki felt a shiver of un-known origin tingle its way up her spine.

'How's Francesca?' she asked suddenly.

He tensed immediately and his face was like granite when he turned around to capture her in a cold, dark stare.

'Do you care?'

'Of course I care! She was my best friend—before you pulled her out of school and forbade me ever to see her again!'

He raised his eyebrows. 'That was a decision I have never regretted. I did not approve of the company she was keeping.'

Suki lifted her chin. 'By that I suppose you mean me?'

He gave her a steady look. 'Yes, Suki—I mean you.'

'The bad influence,' she observed acidly.

He gave a low laugh. 'Precisely. I had no intention of letting my sister start copying the kind of behaviour you were indulging in. Young girls are notoriously affected by what their peers do. And whilst you might have considered it perfectly normal to sleep around I had no intention of letting Francesca do the same.'

Sick at heart, Suki turned away from those dark, intent, judgemental eyes. He still thought of her as nothing more than a tramp—so why bother defending herself? Indeed, how could she possibly defend herself when he spoke nothing more than the truth?

'Is that what you've come here for?' she asked bitterly. 'To go over the past? You've made it clear what you think of me—not that I care what you think any more—'

'Did you ever?' he interrupted softly. 'Or was I just one more virile male for you to wrap those beautiful legs around?'

Suki hesitated painfully, the cruel censure behind his words making the erotic image they created disintegrate immediately. Her amber eyes glittered as she found herself speaking without bothering to analyse her words. 'Of course I cared! You were the older brother of my dearest friend—I was a guest in your house, and you threw me out! Hustled me away like some criminal—flown away at high speed, my holiday cut short. Having to explain to my mother...'

A look almost of pain crossed his face. 'What,' he said, very softly, 'did you tell your mother?'

Her eyes were amber ice. 'Oh, don't worry,' she told him scornfully. 'Your telephone call to her managed to allay any worries she might have had. I don't know how you managed it, but you certainly sweet-talked her into thinking that everything was just fine and dandy. I certainly wasn't going to enlighten her with the truth—that you kicked me out of your bed and out of your house within a few hours!'

*'Dio!'* he swore raggedly. 'Must you put it quite so—crudely?'

'I'm sorry if it's *crude*,' she said deliberately. 'But it's the truth. It's horrible, it's something I'd rather forget—and I will tell you for the last time that I'm simply not interested in rehashing the past—if that's why you've come.'

He stared at her for a long moment of consideration before shaking his head. 'That isn't why I've come,' he told her.

'What, then?' she asked him in bewilderment.

'I've come to ask you to do something for me,' he said simply, but as she was caught up in his direct stare the substance of his words drifted away like gossamer on a breeze because the soft, dark blaze of his eyes had the power to confuse her, to merge the years and send her mind racing back to a time almost eight years ago— the first time she had ever set eyes on Pasquale Caliandro...

# CHAPTER TWO

'ARE you sure they won't mind?' asked Suzanna hesitantly as, with a flick of charcoal, she completed the small portrait she'd been doing of her friend, just as the plane began to make its final descent towards Rome airport.

'Who?' Francesca was too busy batting her eyelashes outrageously at the uniformed male flight attendant to pay much attention to her schoolfriend.

'Your family, of course.' Suzanna flicked her pale auburn plait back over her shoulder. 'It's very kind of them to invite me to stay with them.'

Francesca shrugged. 'They don't care who I invite—they're never around. Papà's always working and is away a lot on business, and my stepmother's away in Paris, apparently. She'll probably be trawling the streets looking for gigolos—'

'Francesca!' exclaimed Suzanna in shocked horror. 'You're not serious?'

'Aren't I?' queried Francesca with unfamiliar bitterness. 'She's twenty years younger than my father. She spends his money like water, and she flirts with anything in a pair of trousers,' she finished, in disgust.

'So why does he stay with her, then?' asked Suzanna softly.

22

'Because she's beautiful. Why else...?' Francesca's voice tailed off momentarily, and when she spoke again it was with her customary, rather sardonic verve. 'Which only leaves big brother—and he's worse than any jailer. But at least with you there you can be my alibi.'

'Alibi?' echoed Suzanna uncertainly.

'Sure.' Francesca's dark eyes flashed. 'He tries to stop me going out with boys, so I don't tell him any more. And if he asks *you* anything, then you tell him you last saw me praying in church!'

'Francesca!' said Suzanna uneasily because she didn't know sometimes whether to take her effervescent friend seriously, and her fingers began to pleat the hem of her white dress nervously. 'You know you don't mean that!'

'I know that going home for the holidays is going to cramp my style,' muttered Francesca. 'The discos I go to during term-time are *fantastic*—I wish you'd come along too.'

Suzanna shook her head. 'Discos aren't really my thing.' In discos she felt gangly, awkward. And when you stood at almost six feet in your stockinged feet that was inevitable.

'That's because you've never given them a chance!' Francesca's attention was caught by the thumbnail sketch in Suzanna's hand. 'Hey! That's good—it's me, isn't it?'

'Do you like it?' smiled Suzanna.

'Yeah. May I keep it?'

'Sure.'

The plane was coming in to land, and there was little time for talking again until they were seated in the back of the shiny, chaffeur-driven limousine and heading towards the Caliandro mansion. Francesca spent the entire journey chattering as she freed Suzanna's hair from her plaits and teased it into a blazing and magnificent furnace of waves, and Suzanna was so enraptured at the spectacular landscape passing them by that the subject of alibis was all but forgotten.

Suzanna and Francesca were both at finishing school in Switzerland. 'It's bound to finish me off sooner or later!' Francesca always joked. It was the expensive kind of school which was intended to produce young ladies. Daughters of the rich and the noble attended, most of them from privileged but broken homes.

Suzanna's own father had died, leaving a wife, a son and a daughter, and a car-manufacturing plant which her brother had over-ambitious plans for. Money was tight, but a savings plan taken out at her birth had ensured that at least Suzanna's expensive education would be paid for. But she worried about her mother's well-being, and she worried about her feckless brother, Piers, being in charge of the family business...

Francesca's own mother had died a few years back, and her father had quickly remarried. A mistake, according to Francesca, and it seemed that there was little love lost between her and her stepmother. 'And my brother really *hates* her!' she'd added. 'He can hardly bear to be in the same room as her.'

It didn't sound like a very *happy* house, thought Suzanna suddenly.

Francesca's voice broke into her thoughts. 'We're here!' she exclaimed as the car swept down a gravelled drive and came to a halt in front of an imposing white building, and then her voice dropped to a dramatic whisper. 'And here comes Pasquale, my brother—so don't forget—if he asks whether I date men you just tell him that I've shown bags of disinterest!'

Through the window of the limousine, Suzanna could see the most handsome man she had ever set eyes on, and her heart lurched painfully in her chest. She blinked several times, as if afraid that she'd simply dreamt him up.

Quite unbelievably, she hadn't.

He was tall—quite spectacularly tall for a man of Italian origin. His shoulders were strong and wide and his hips were narrow. His nose was a proud Roman curve and his eyes were dark and glittering. For Suzanna, naïve and unused to men, the experience of staring up into the face of Francesca's brother was like something out of the romantic novels she'd read since her early teens; she looked, and was, completely smitten.

Afterwards, she was to tell herself that she had been ripe to fall for someone—*any*one. It was just unfortunate that it had happened to be Pasquale...

He greeted his sister with a kiss on both cheeks and then held his hand out formally to Suzanna.

The sun was behind her and seemed to create a halo of golden-red around her hair—or so

Francesca whispered to her later that night when Suzanna's heart was still pounding in that strange, unfamiliar way which hadn't left her since she'd first set eyes on Pasquale.

The short white cheesecloth dress she wore merely hinted at the outline of the smooth young flesh which lay beneath, but when he looked at her a stillness and a watchfulness came over Pasquale Caliandro. He caught her small hand in his firm, warm and masculine grip and as she gave him a look of helpless fascination his eyes narrowed, his mouth hardening as he stared down at her.

'I think my brother fancies you,' Francesca said that night as they got ready for bed. 'He gave you a real mean, hungry look!'

'Rubbish!' said Suzanna, blushing furiously.

Of course it was rubbish, she convinced herself as she dived into the pool one morning, a few days after she'd arrived. Men who fancied you didn't virtually ignore you in a way which she thought bordered on downright rudeness. And they certainly didn't speak to you in that awful, brusque way he had of addressing her. One day he'd actually had the *nerve* to tell her to stop hanging her head and to be proud of her height!

Sometimes, she thought as she ploughed up and down the swimming pool in an effort to get rid of the heat in her veins which just wouldn't go away—sometimes she thought that Pasquale almost *disliked* her—his manner towards her was so abrupt.

And yet at others...

She shivered. Other times she would turn around to find him watching her. Just watching her with a dark and brooding intensity which frightened the life out of her, yet thrilled her at the same time.

Just about the only nice thing he'd said to her had been when he'd found her sketching quietly in the garden one day.

He had stood silently looking over her shoulder for at least a minute, and had given a little nod as he'd watched her long fingers cleverly re-creating the glass summer house, which was overhung with vines.

'That's good,' he observed. 'Good enough to make it your career, I think.' And Suzanna had blushed furiously at the unexpected praise.

She turned on her back and lazily kicked her legs around in the cool water. It was indeed a strange household she was staying with, she reflected. Francesca seemed to spend her whole time concocting schemes to get to one of the discotheques in the city, but so far she hadn't succeeded, since Pasquale vehemently blocked every suggestion. 'You're far too young,' he'd told her emphatically, and then his eyes had narrowed and he had given Suzanna one of his rare looks. 'Do you girls go to many discos?' he'd queried, his dark eyes suspicious.

'Never!' Suzanna and Francesca had replied in unison, but Suzanna hadn't been able to stop herself from blushing at Francesca's easy lie, and she was certain that Pasquale's sharp eyes had noticed, for he'd frowned severely.

Francesca and Pasquale's father she hardly saw at all. A still handsome man of sixty, with streaks of silver in his dark hair, he seemed to spend most of the time working—as Francesca had prophesied—making it home only in time for the evening meal. Usually at dinner it was just the three of them, as Pasquale always seemed to be out on a date with one of the many glamorous-sounding women who telephoned him, and their stepmother was still in Paris.

But today Suzanna was alone in the house. Pasquale was working and Signor Caliandro had flown to Naples for the day. Francesca had gone to visit her godmother on the other side of the city. She'd invited Suzanna to go along, but Suzanna knew that the elderly lady spoke little English and had decided that it would be fairer to let Francesca go alone. Besides, she rather liked having this luxurious house to herself.

The swimming pool was vast and deliciously cool and Suzanna dived to the depths of the turquoise water and swam around. She'd almost used up all her air, when the devastatingly sharp pain of cramp stabbed ruthlessly at her calf.

Perhaps if she'd had a lungful of air and hadn't been near the bottom of the pool she wouldn't have panicked, but panic she did, doing the worst thing she could possibly have done—she gulped water down, her arms and legs flailing wildly in all directions.

Her head and chest felt as though they might actually burst, but suddenly she felt a pair of hands tightly grasping her waist. She tried instinctively to wriggle free, but whoever was holding her had an indomitable strength and would not let her go.

She found herself being propelled to the surface, where her mouth broke open and greedily sucked in air, and she fell back against the chest of her rescuer, a solid, hard wall of muscle, but she knew without turning to look at him that it was Pasquale.

His arms were still around her waist, and his head dropped briefly to rest on hers.

'*Dio!*' he exclaimed savagely, and kicked off and swam towards the pool steps. He climbed out first, then picked her up easily and carried her to lay her down on the soft, sun-warmed grass.

She realised that he had dived in fully dressed—that he had not even bothered to kick off his beautiful, soft, handmade shoes, which were now sodden. His silk shirt clung to him like a second skin and his sopping trousers now etched every hard sinew of the strong shafts of his powerful thighs.

His eyes were blazing. 'You fool! You crazy little *idiot*!' he cried out, and he ran his hands thoroughly but dispassionately over her body, like a doctor examining for broken bones.

'I—I'm sorry.' She trembled as her body felt his warm, sure touch.

'And so you should be!' he told her furiously. 'Don't you realise that you could have drowned?' His eyes narrowed as he took in her white, frightened face. 'Do you hurt anywhere?' he demanded.

Humiliatingly, her teeth stared to chatter so that she couldn't speak.

'Do you?' he demanded again, still in that same grim tone. 'Hurt anywhere? Tell me!'

She couldn't cope with his harshness, not when she was feeling so vulnerable, and she did what she hadn't done since her father had died the previous year—she burst into tears.

Instantly, his attitude altered. He looked appalled with himself as he gathered her into his arms and laid his strong hand protectively against the back of her head.

'Don't cry, *bella mia*,' he whispered. 'There is no need for tears. You are safe now.'

But the shock of realising what might have happened if he had not been there made her sob all the harder, and he made a little sound, a small, rough assertion beneath his breath, as he picked her up and carried her towards the house. She was too weak to do anything other than rest her head against his chest, and gradually the sobs receded. It was just like visiting heaven, being in his arms like this, she realised, her body all wet and clingy and close. She could have stayed like that all day.

'Wh-where are you taking me?' she wondered aloud as he mounted the stairs.

'To get you dry,' he answered. His gentleness had vanished, and he spoke again in that grim, terse tone which left her wondering why he still seemed so angry with her.

He carried her to her own room and set her down on the thick carpet, glancing quickly around, his eyes narrowing as they alighted on a tiny pair of knickers which were lying in an open drawer, together with a matching bra.

Suzanna blushed.

'Do you have a towelling robe?' he asked.

She shook her head. A towelling robe wasn't the kind of thing you brought to Italy in the middle of summer. She only had a silk wrap.

'You'd better wait here!' he told her, and left the bedroom.

He returned minutes later with what was obviously his own robe—a luxurious, almost velvety towelling garment in a deep, midnight-blue colour—and threw it down on the bed. 'Now strip off,' he told her. 'Completely. Put the robe on and I will run you a bath.'

If any other man had issued such a curt and intimate order, Suzanna would have screamed for the police, but because it was Pasquale she simply nodded obediently. He set off for the *en suite* without a backward glance, his shoulders curiously stiff and set, and Suzanna began to do as he had told her.

Easier said than done. She'd never thought that it would be so difficult to remove two tiny scraps of bikini, but the wet material was clinging to her cold, damp skin and her fingers were stiff and trembling with the cold.

So when, minutes later, the bathroom door opened and Pasquale came back in, accompanied by clouds of delicious-looking, scented steam, it was to find her almost sobbing with frustration as she attempted to slide her hands round to her back to unclip the clasp of her bikini-top.

There was a moment when he froze, as though he'd never seen a woman almost naked before—but that was nonsense. Francesca had already regaled her with stories of Pasquale smuggling girls out of his room when he was still at boarding-school. And you only had to look at that brooding, almost dangerous physique to know that Pasquale would have tasted most of the pleasures of lovemaking...

A strange look crossed those tight features. A look of anger, but of something else too—something which even the totally innocent Suzanna recognised as desire—and then he said something very softly and very eloquently in Italian, before moving quickly to her side.

'I...I'm sorry,' she mumbled. 'I can't... My fingers are all...'

He shook his head, said not a word but deftly undid the clasp with a single fluid movement that sent a brief spear of jealousy through her as she found herself imagining those strong, bronzed hands undressing other women too. Her unfettered breasts bounced free and she heard him catch his breath on a muffled, almost savage note.

He almost flung the robe over her and swiftly knotted the belt around her narrow waist, and then he knelt at her feet, his hands moving inside the robe until they were on her bare hips. Suzanna held her breath with dazed and exultant shock as she felt the heat of his fingers on her cool flesh, but he kept his eyes averted as he peeled the damp bottoms off all the way down the slender length of her thighs, and her cold and discomfort vanished completely as she felt the brief slide of his hand against her inner thigh.

Something hot and potent and powerful bubbled its way into life in her veins as rapidly as bush-fire, and Suzanna was racked with an uncontrollable shudder as she became sexually aware of her body for the first time in her life.

Had he seen her automatic response to his touch? Was that why his mouth had twisted into that harsh, almost frightening line? Why the hard glittering of his dark eyes now transformed him into some unforgettable but slightly forbidding stranger?

'Now get in the bath,' he said roughly, and he tossed the bikini away from him as though it had been contaminated. He rose to his feet and moved towards the door, but without his customary elegance and fluidity of motion. 'And be out of there in twenty minutes—no longer,' he ordered, but then a wry note which bordered on amusement entered his voice and, thankfully, removed some of the awful tension from the air. 'No falling asleep is permitted! Understand?' he finished softly.

'Yes, Pasquale,' she answered meekly.

'Good. I'll be downstairs making you some coffee.'

She wandered into the bathroom in a heady daze, wrapped in the thickness of his robe, reluctant to remove it because the scent of it—of *him*—was just too heavenly for words. She hugged her arms against her breasts, then wiped away some of the steam from the mirror and stared into it, mesmerised by the heightened colour of her cheeks and the strange, almost feverish glitter in her eyes.

But what was she imagining? That he had been as affected by that brief encounter as she had? Pasquale Caliandro, the toast of Rome, bothered by a schoolgirl?

No way! she thought with honest reluctance as she pulled off the robe and stepped into the fragrant, steamy water.

The bath made her feel almost normal again. She washed her hair and left it hanging loose, dressing in a pair of white jeans and a loose white cotton sweater before going downstairs to find Pasquale, and the coffee.

She stood in the doorway watching him, enjoying the sight of such a very masculine man looking so thoroughly at ease in the domestic domain of the kitchen.

His dark eyes flicked over her impassively. 'Feeling better?' he enquired.

Physically, yes, certainly. But there was still that tingling awareness fizzing around her veins which his touch had brought to life. 'Much better,' she answered politely, and then her gratitude came out in a rush. 'I wanted to thank you, Pasquale—for...' it sounded a bit over the top to say it, but say it she must '...saving my life,' she gulped.

He shook his head and smiled gently. 'Let's forget it.'

But she would never forget it, she knew that, and the burgeoning, almost schoolgirlish attraction she had felt towards Pasquale suddenly flowered and blossomed into mature life.

I'm in love with him, she thought, with a calm certainty.

'Sit down,' he offered, and she drew up one of the tall stools he'd indicated and sat, leaning her elbows on the counter as she struggled to say something which didn't involve the fact that he'd seen her half-naked just minutes ago. Sitting there, with her still damp hair and her face completely bare of make-up, she suddenly felt very young and very boring.

'You look very efficient in the kitchen!' she remarked brightly. 'I'm surprised!'

He raised his dark eyebrows fractionally, but didn't comment on the sexism inherent in her remark; instead he began to pour the fragrant brew into a large porcelain cup. 'The Italian male is renowned for many things, but not, I think, for his prowess in the kitchen,' he said as he pushed the cup towards her.

She knew that. She knew, too, exactly what they *were* renowned for... For being wonderful...lovers... She gulped, and took a deep breath. 'So you decided to break with tradition?' she joked.

A sudden bleakness dulled the magnificent eyes as he added sugar to his own cup. 'Unhappily, yes. One cannot have servants on hand every minute of the day, and when my mother died . . .' He hesitated. 'Well, Papà was in a state of shock for such a long time, and Francesca was too young . . .'

Suzanna could have kicked herself for her blundering insensitivity. 'Oh, Lord,' she groaned softly. 'I didn't mean to put my foot in it.'

He gave a small smile. 'Time gives a certain immunity against pain, Suzanna.' And his accent deepened. 'Didn't your own father die very suddenly?'

Suzanna went very quiet. 'Francesca told you?'

'Yes.' He paused, and the dark eyes were very direct. 'It was a car crash, I believe?'

If it had been anyone else but him, she suspected that she would have found the question a gross intrusion, but Pasquale asking it seemed like the most natural thing in the world. 'Yes,' she said, and swallowed.

'You were thinking of him by the pool—when you began to cry?'

His perception quite took her breath away. 'How on earth could you know that?'

'I know quite well the difference between shock and grief. And bottling it up won't help, you know.' He gave her a gentle smile. 'Now drink your coffee and I will take you out for lunch. Will that cheer you up?'

'*Lunch?*' She felt like Cinderella. 'Are you sure?'

His mouth moved in an enigmatic smile. 'Quite sure,' he said drily. 'You see, another characteristic of Italian men is their enjoyment of being seen with an exceptionally beautiful young lady.'

She knew that he had deliberately emphasised the young bit, but she didn't care. Pasquale was taking her for lunch and that was all that mattered.

In the event, that lunch ruined her for every future meal of her life. He took her to a lovely restaurant, and he was charm personified. The food was delicious and the half-glass of wine he allowed her incomparable. He seemed so at home in the discreetly elegant surroundings, and she tried to emulate his cool confidence. The down side was that at least three women came over to greet him—women with stacks more experience and poise than Suzanna—and she found herself wishing that they might totter and trip on the ridiculously high heels they all seemed to be wearing!

It was past three when they drove back, and she felt warm and contented and wondered what he would suggest doing that afternoon. But he did not get out of the car.

'I will leave you to amuse yourself,' he told her, and he gave her a stern look. 'But please—no more swimming—not today!'

She found it hard to hide the disappointment. 'But where are you going?'

'To work. Be so kind as to tell Papà and Francesca that I shall be late—and that I shall not be in for supper.'

Suzanna felt as flat as a pancake as she walked slowly back into the flower-covered villa. She spent the rest of the afternoon trying to write a letter, but it was difficult, because outside a wind was insidiously whipping up, while in the distance she heard the ominous rumble of thunder.

She began to long for the return of the others, but no one came back. No Francesca or Signor Caliandro. The villa suddenly seemed awfully big and awfully empty with just her and the cook, who was busy in the kitchen.

Francesca rang at six to say that she would be staying at her godmother's. 'The storm is very bad here,' she explained. 'And it's moving down towards your part of the city. Will you be all right? Is Pasquale or Papà back yet?'

Suzanna didn't want to worry her friend, so she didn't bother telling her that Pasquale was not in for supper and that there was no sign of her father.

She decided to keep herself busy, and there were enough adult toys in that house to amuse anyone—rows of film classics in the room where the video and large viewing screen were kept and a whole library of books, with an English section which would have kept an avid reader going for years.

So Suzanna passed the rest of the day amusing herself as best she could. She gave herself a manicure and a pedicure. She borrowed Francesca's tongs and made her curls hang in brightly coloured corkscrews.

The cook was clearly worried about the weather, and so Suzanna told her to go home early.

But later, as she perched upon the stool in the kitchen, eating the chicken and salad which had been prepared for supper, Suzanna could hear the distant rumbling of the storm growing in intensity.

At the best of times she wasn't fond of storms, but when she was marooned and isolated in a large villa in a strange country—well...

She went around securing the windows as the wind began to howl like a hungry animal outside, and the rain spattered and thundered in huge, unforgiving drops against the glass.

She was sitting up in bed reading a book, when the room was plunged into darkness and she screamed aloud at the unexpected blackness which enveloped her like a suffocating blanket.

She tried to reason with herself that it was just a power-cut, not unusual in a storm of this ferocity, but it was no good—she began to scream anew as a branch hurled itself against the window-pane, like an intruder banging to come inside.

She didn't know how long she lay there, cowering with fear, but suddenly she felt the cover being whipped back and there stood Pasquale, his clothes spattered with rain, his dark, luxuriant hair plastered to his beautifully shaped head.

He took hold of her shoulders and levered her up towards him to stare down intently into her face.

'You're OK?' he asked succinctly for the second time that day, and she nodded tremulously.

'Sure?'

'Yes.'

'Where are the others?'

'Francesca says the storm's too bad to travel back. I don't know about your father.'

'They've closed the airport,' he said briefly, and then his eyes softened. 'Were you very frightened here, on your own?'

Bravado made her lie. 'Not—really,' she said in a small voice, but as she stared up at him all in her world suddenly felt very, very safe.

'Wait here,' he told her. 'Don't move. I'm going to try to do something about the lights.'

She had no intention of going *anywhere*! So she sank back obediently against the pillows until she heard him calling her, then leapt out of bed to find him outside the door, holding a candelabra in his hand, with three flickering candles casting strange, enticing shadows onto his face. He looked like someone who had stepped out of a painting; someone from another age, she thought fleetingly.

'Come downstairs and get warm,' he said, and she followed him downstairs, watching while he built a fire and fetched two brandies, which he placed on a small table in front of the roaring blaze.

He'd changed, she noticed. Gone was the sodden suit, replaced by a black cashmere sweater and black jeans. On his feet he wore nothing, and she couldn't help noticing how beautifully shaped his toes were. Imagine even finding someone's feet attractive! She really *was* in a bad way! Her mouth dried and her heart thundered as he looked up from the logs and answered her shy smile almost reluctantly.

'Brandy?' he asked coolly.

She remembered him policing her at lunchtime and allowing her only half a glass of wine, and perhaps he remembered it too, because he laughed.

'It's purely for medicinal purposes. You look white and shocked to me. This has been quite a day for you, Suzanna.'

It would sound extremely naïve to say she'd never tried brandy before, wouldn't it? she thought. Besides which, his words were accurate enough, and she *felt* shocked. 'I'd love some,' she agreed, and sat on the rug, holding her hands out towards the blaze.

The brandy was hot and bitter-sweet in her throat, but she felt its effect stealing over her immediately, and she wriggled her toes as the warmth invaded her.

'Feeling better now?' he asked.

'*Mmm!* Much!' She briefly closed her eyes and gave a blissful smile and when she opened them again it was to find him staring at her intently, something unfathomable written on his face, and, quite suddenly, he got to his feet.

'Bedtime,' he said abruptly, in a firm voice. 'It's late. I'll tidy up down here—you go on up. Here, take this candle, but don't leave it lit.'

But Suzanna couldn't sleep. Outside the storm raged, but inside her own storm was raging. She recalled the feel of his arms as he'd carried her upstairs from the pool. The feel of those firm hands freeing her breasts, removing the bikini.

Restlessly, she tossed and turned, until she gave up the whole idea of trying to sleep. She decided to go in search of some matches to light the candle and read her book.

She pulled on her silken wrap and silently made her way downstairs to the kitchen, and after a bit of hunting around she found the matches she was after.

She was just creeping back along the corridor towards her bedroom when a dark figure loomed up in front of her and she almost collided with Pasquale.

He wore black silk pyjama trousers and nothing else. She found her eyes drawn to the beautiful breadth of his hair-roughened chest. His dark hair was ruffled and his chin shadowed in the strange yellow light of the storm.

'What are you doing creeping around the house?' he demanded in a voice which managed to sound both dangerous and soft, his eyes briefly flicking to the rise and fall of her breasts beneath their thin layer of silk. 'Why aren't you in bed?'

He made it sound as if she'd been committing some sort of crime. 'Because I couldn't sleep,' she told him defensively.

There was a moment's silence, broken only by the harsh sound of his breathing. 'Neither could I,' he said eventually, and then his voice softened. 'Does the sound of the storm frighten you?'

She nodded. 'A little.'

'There is nothing to be frightened of,' he said, and with his hand in the small of her back he propelled her along to her bedroom door. 'Don't you know that it's simply the gods clapping their hands? Didn't they tell you that when you were a little girl?'

But at that moment an enormous clap of thunder seemed to rock the very foundations of the house, and Suzanna jumped in fright.

'Get into bed,' he told her brusquely.

She did as he asked, but her eyes were huge in her face as she stared up at him in mute appeal.

He shook his head. 'No, Suzanna. No. You don't know what it is you're asking,' he told her obliquely.

She hadn't really been aware that she was asking anything, but now it dawned on her that she wanted him to stay. She wanted him to shield her from the elements which raged outside.

And those within? she wondered briefly.

She heard his reluctant sigh.

'Very well—I'll sit here until you fall asleep,' he said in an oddly resigned kind of voice.

Suzanna slithered down beneath the duvet, hearing the slow, steady thump of her heart beating loudly in her ears.

Pasquale sat on the edge of the bed, as far away from her as possible. 'Now sleep,' he urged softly. 'Nothing can hurt you while I am here.'

She awoke to find herself wrapped tightly in his arms beneath the duvet, her head resting on his shoulder while he slept. She heard the comforting steadiness of his breathing, and, acting purely on the instincts of one who was only half-awake, she nestled even closer into his embrace. He tightened his arms around her, and she had never felt so cosseted or so safe in her whole life. She let her head drift down so that her cheek lay on his bare chest and she could hear his heart beating loud and steady as a drum.

She couldn't resist it; she simply couldn't help herself. Lifting her mouth, she kissed his neck, and he sighed and stirred, his hand moving lazily from her waist to cup her breast over the thin silk of her nightdress, finding its tip and inciting it into immediate tingling life, stroke by glorious stroke.

He began to kiss her neck as he unbuttoned the nightdress and slowly bared her breasts, murmuring all the while in his native tongue.

She didn't understand what he was saying to her, but she could hear the pleasure in his voice, the soft lilt of the seductive Italian language sounding almost like poetry. And then he began to kiss the tip of one breast, and she shuddered as his hand moved down to begin to slide the silky material of her nightdress up over her knees.

He started to kiss her mouth, long and hard and deeply, and Suzanna opened her lips to him as though she had been born knowing how he wanted her to kiss him back.

She heard him give a low, husky laugh, a cross between appraisal and stark hunger, as his hand began to tantalisingly stroke the sensitive skin of her inner thigh, and a moan of delight was dragged from her lips as he sent her desire soaring out of control, and she moved restlessly against him.

He gave another low laugh then moved her hand down over his chest to the waistband of those black silk pyjama trousers which did absolutely nothing to conceal his arousal, uttering something low and fervent against her ear as he did so.

Her Italian was sketchy, but she knew what he meant—his hands showed her what he meant and the urgent appeal in his voice made his meaning as clear as if he had spoken it in English. *Undress me.*

She had been born for this. She gave a whimper of pleasure as she slid her hand inside the waistband, knowing instinctively and without shyness exactly what he wanted her to do. Her slender hand captured the swollen silky shaft, her fingers moving delicately up and down, and she revelled in the small sound he made in the back of his throat.

Suddenly urgent, he peeled the nightdress off her body, and she suddenly realised where all this was leading. He was going to make love to her.

Right now.

His eyes were slitted as his hand slid under her head and he bent his own to dazzle her with a storm of kisses which had her almost sobbing with pleasure. She loved him—yes, she did. She would die for him.

'Oh, Pasquale,' she whispered ecstatically. *'Pasquale.'*

He stilled at her words. She realised that they were the first she had spoken, and it was as if they had been in the midst of some erotic spell which had been shattered into smithereens by that helpless little plea.

His eyes snapped wide open, and he stared down at her face with a look of growing horror.

She saw the struggle echoed in his features as his mind obviously sought for supremacy over his body, and there was one moment when she thought that his mind had lost—when his furious gaze strayed to her swollen breasts, and she felt him move, was certain that he was going to just impale her, take her there and then, regardless.

But the moment passed.

He pushed himself away from her as though she were something unspeakably distasteful, and the look of undisguised disgust on his face shook her to the core.

He waited until he had roughly pulled his pyjama trousers back on with unsteady hands before he turned round, and his face was as cold as marble.

'You manipulative little...!' His words tailed off then he whispered, also in English—just to make sure that she understood every damning word he spoke—'You scheming little temptress—with your come-to-bed eyes and your bright hair and your perfumed body! Do you know that men talk of women like you? Yes, and sometimes they even dream of them. You're every man's fantasy—ripe and willing and eager.

'But do you know something, Suzanna? It leaves a bitter taste in my mouth to have almost lain with someone who has such little regard for her body.' His mouth twisted. 'Dear *God*!' he said in disgust as he shook his dark head in disbelief. 'You're barely seventeen! When the hell did you start?'

She had to lie there and take it for what choice did she have? She could just imagine his scornful disbelief if she tried to tell him she was a virgin, particularly after the way she'd just behaved. What defence for her wayward behaviour could she possibly have? And to tell him that she believed herself to be in love with him would be to heap even more scorn down about her.

He paced the room and came back to stare down at her, and by now every last trace of passion had vanished. To judge by his expression, he had about as much regard for her as he would for a squashed insect.

'And this is the kind of woman I have allowed my sister to associate with!' he thundered. 'To bring into my home! No wonder her end-of-term report was of such an appallingly low standard. No wonder she is seemingly obsessed with discos and with boys.' His dark eyes looked almost black with condemnation as he studied her with icy distaste.

And Suzanna, who had opened her mouth to protest at being condemned out of hand as the bad influence on Francesca, shut it quickly, knowing that she could now say nothing. She certainly couldn't drop her friend in it by sug-

gesting that Francesca was her own woman, and
that Suzanna was the *last* person to influence her
in wild ways.

And, loyalty apart, he wouldn't believe her.
Why should he? She had behaved in a way which
was already beginning to make her cringe, as she
remembered just what she had been doing with
him, and what she had been prepared to do with
him...

'No defence?' he quizzed softly.

Suzanna bit her lip and turned her head away,
but he moved forward with the lissomeness and
stealth of some threatening jungle cat to capture
her chin in his olive-skinned hand and turn it to
face him, so that she was trapped in the blazing
hostility of his stare. 'Listen to me, and listen to
me carefully,' he said, in a voice as dangerously
soft as it was possible to imagine, and Suzanna
felt herself shivering as she registered that touch,
that searing look. 'I want you packed and ready
to leave this house by six tomorrow morning—'

'But I—'

'Shut *up*,' he told her callously. 'You will do
as I say. I want you ready to leave by six. I will
have a car take you to the airport, and you will
be put on the first available flight to England,
where I will arrange to have a car meet you and
take you to your home. I'm assuming that your
mother is at home?'

'Yes,' she said miserably. 'But what on earth
am I going to tell her?'

For a moment he hesitated, but it was just a
moment, before the contempt hardened his fea-

tures once more. 'Leave that to me,' he said harshly. 'I will ring her and tell her that Francesca and I have to go away unexpectedly. Which is true,' he added grimly, 'since I intend spending some time alone with my sister to teach her just what is and what is not acceptable behaviour in a young woman.' And with a final withering look he strode towards the door, where he paused briefly.

'Oh, and there's one other thing,' he said softly.

She wondered just what else he could throw at her.

'Don't *ever* attempt to contact my sister again. You are to have nothing to do with the Caliandro family ever again. Is that understood?'

Suzanna lifted her chin in a show of pride she was far from feeling. 'Perfectly,' she said, in a voice that was so steady that she marvelled at it. But now that he was no longer in such close proximity normal reasoning began to assert itself, and she seized with delight on the fundamental flaw in his stern lecture to her about morals.

Her eyes sparked with their own danger. 'But surely you don't imagine that you can heap all the blame for what just happened at *my* feet, Pasquale,' she told him quietly, and she saw the sudden tension in his body. 'It does, as they say, take two,' she added coolly. 'And you were, after all, the one who instigated it.'

'Oh, was I?' he mocked.

She blushed, but she didn't flinch from the accusation in his stare. 'If the idea of making love

to me so appalled you, then you could have
stopped a lot sooner than you did.'

'When a man is aroused like that from sleep,
he doesn't generally go in for analysis.' His face
was like stone, his eyes scornful as he turned to
twist the doorhandle. 'Let's just say that I
mistook you for somebody else,' he added
insultingly.

And as Suzanna looked at that dark, furious
figure retreating from her bedroom she thought
that she had never, ever hated anyone so much
in her whole life.

# CHAPTER THREE

THE mists of memory cleared and Suki found herself standing in the room staring at Pasquale, trying to remind herself that seven years had passed, and that this man had hurt her as badly as she could ever have imagined being hurt.

Though in a way she had Pasquale to thank for her startling transformation from chrysalis to butterfly. After the humiliation of her experience with him, she'd felt that nothing could ever possibly hurt her that much again. Her shyness had become a thing of the past. From gawky Suzanna, the new Suki had emerged, with a brand-new, slightly brittle exterior which would guarantee that she would never get hurt like that again.

Remember that, she thought as she stared at the man in front of her.

She had known him when he was twenty-four and he had been utterly devastating. Seven years on and that charm and charisma was even more potent, and Pasquale at thirty-one had acquired a lazy arrogance which she was quickly discovering she was not immune to...

Protectively, she pulled a silk wrap on over her bikini, and saw his mouth harden.

51

'I cannot believe that the years have made you so shy,' he mocked, 'when once you flaunted your body so proudly for me to see!'

She decided to ignore that; getting into a fight with him would give him the opportunity to defeat her, and that was something she would never allow to happen. Not again. 'So what do you want to talk to me about, Pasquale?' she asked coolly as she picked up a hairbrush from the mantelpiece and began to drag it through her heavy silken waves of pale auburn hair.

His dark eyes penetrated her. 'How long have you known Salvatore Bruni?'

Suki's mouth opened in amazement as he said the name of the photographer who had brought her here. 'You know him too?'

He arrogantly ignored her question. 'I said— how long have you known him for?' he repeated ominously.

She lifted her chin defiantly, outraged at the heavy-handed tone he was using. 'I really don't think that's any of your business.'

'Let me be the judge of that!' His eyes narrowed. 'Tell me,' he said, very softly, 'are you congenitally programmed to only have affairs with men who belong to other women?'

Suki stared at him, genuine bewilderment in her eyes. 'I don't know what you're talking about.'

He stared at her in silence for a few moments, as if weighing up whether or not her perplexity was genuine.

'Salvatore Bruni, the man you are currently having an affair with, just happens to be engaged to my secretary. I had a phone call from her late last night—she was sobbing her heart out because he had gone away for the weekend with one of the world's most beautiful women without bothering to tell her. A woman, moreover, whose reputation with men goes before her.' His eyes glittered ominously. 'Even if I did not have firsthand experience of it myself,' he concluded softly.

Suki's world spun. 'I don't happen to be *having* an affair with Salvatore, actually,' she told him frostily. 'He's taking photos of me for a book he's doing. We happen to be here *working*.'

He gave her a cold stare. 'Oh, really?' he drawled disbelievingly, and his eyes roved around the room, coming to rest pointedly on an old pair of faded jeans—and very obviously a man's pair of jeans—which were lying in a heap on the chair beside the bed.

Suki flushed in horror, realising how incriminating those wretched jeans looked. Beneath her exquisite exterior she was a born *hausfrau* and she happened to be very nifty with a needle. So when Salvatore had torn his jeans she had automatically offered to sew them for him. 'Oh, those,' she said, stung into defending herself, aware that Pasquale was eyeing her stained cheeks critically. 'Yes, they belong to Salvatore. I promised to mend them for him. They got ripped.'

'I can imagine.' He laughed cynically. 'In your eagerness to tear them from his body, no doubt?'

Suki swallowed down the lump of distaste in her throat. 'He ripped them on a rock while we were shooting at the beach this morning, if you *must* know!'

'And so you're going to sew them for him, are you?' he asked in a voice of deadly saccharin. 'How sweetly domestic.' And then his voice hardened into a threat. 'But, as I told you before, he's engaged to someone else. So just keep those beautiful little hands off him, will you, Suki?'

Oh, the sins of her past. Was her one youthful misdemeanour going to damn her for ever in his eyes? 'Are you suggesting that I'd go on holiday with a man if I knew that he was engaged to someone else?' she snapped.

He shrugged. 'Why not? We established a long time ago that you have very little in the way of morals. Nothing would surprise me about you in the sexual stakes, *bella mia*.'

Why had she permitted him to enter her room in the first place? she wondered wildly. She was no longer a naïve young girl staying in *his* house, subject to *his* whims and orders. 'I did not invite you here to insult me,' she said with fierce determination. 'So if that's all you intend to do you can get out. Right now.'

But he didn't move an inch; there wasn't even a flicker of expression on that hard, implacable face in response. 'I am staying here until I have your word that you will leave Salvatore alone.'

Little did he know that she wouldn't touch Salvatore or any other man—engaged or not— with a bargepole! Men were far more trouble than they were worth! And she might have told him if he'd been anyone other than the man who had trampled all over her tender, youthful emotions. One sight of that coolly confident face telling her to lay off was enough to set her blood boiling.

'I see that you still like to play the puppet-master, Pasquale,' she scorned. 'First you try to run your sister's friendships for her, and now you're meddling in your secretary's love-life. Tell me, do you get some kind of kick out of trying to control people?'

'Sometimes a little intervention is essential,' he stated arrogantly, untouched by her criticism.

'You think so?' She gave him an acid smile. 'Your secretary—what's her name?' she enquired.

He frowned, the dark eyes narrowing dangerously. 'Cristina. Why?'

Suki stared at him. 'Poor Cristina,' she said, shaking her head from side to side.

He continued to frown. 'Poor Cristina?' he repeated.

'Mmm. I mean, it's *terribly* protective of you, but do you really think it's a good thing that she's engaged to a man she patently doesn't trust? A man who takes another woman away to the South of France?'

A muscle ticked ominously in the dark, olive cheek. 'If it was any woman other than you, Suki, then yes, I would certainly be concerned for her future happiness.'

A red flame of fury swam before her eyes. 'And what's that supposed to mean?'

He laughed—a chilly replica of sardonic humour which had the tiny hairs on the back of her head standing up like soldiers. 'Simply that while I do not condone Salvatore's behaviour I find it understandable to some degree. After all, I have been victim to your charms myself.' His voice dropped to a silky caress. 'You see, you are a born Circe. You tempt beyond reason. That beautiful body of yours is born for love, those cat's eyes promise pleasures too manifold to believe. What man could resist such promise? I myself almost succumbed.

'Salvatore is a red-blooded man and Cristina a respectable young woman, both members of the Italian community in New York. Proprieties have naturally been observed. It is not our custom for sex to take place before marriage, and a woman who indulges in such behaviour is not to be respected. Do you get my drift, *cara*?'

Yes, she got his meaning all right, and, though it shouldn't have done—oh, how it hurt! 'Loud and clear,' she murmured, somehow masking her feelings from him. 'You're saying that it's OK for a man to play around before marriage—as long as it's with someone else? And that for the woman there is nothing but the long wait until the matrimonial night?'

'I was right!' he stormed, and in his rage he sounded so very Italian, the American twang in his accent, picked up during his Ivy League college days, light years away. 'Still the alley-cat! What woman would admit to such thoughts?'

'Any woman who's sick of the double standard, I should imagine!' she shouted, aware that she was in danger of ascribing false standards to herself, but she didn't care what he thought of her—she simply *didn't care*! 'How dare you say that a woman must remain as pure as the driven snow, whilst giving a man carte blanche to do exactly as he pleases? That's like saying that men have uncontrollable urges, whilst women can sublimate theirs!'

He was suddenly alert. 'And you don't think that's true, *cara*?' he murmured.

She knew what she *thought*—she just didn't have any experience to back up her words; but Pasquale didn't know that. More importantly, he wouldn't believe it in a hundred years—so what did she have to lose? She raised her chin up and stared at him defiantly, not caring now what she said, only determined that she should rile him. 'No, I don't! I believe in equality! You can't have one rule for men and another one for women. Either they both live by the same rules or you abandon those rules altogether!'

The dark eyes were hooded as they surveyed her. 'And you?' he said softly. 'You have had many lovers, Suki?'

She saw the flash in his eyes, and instinctively, incredulously, she knew what had provoked it. Pasquale was *jealous*! *Jealous*! He had wanted her all those years ago, yes, but he had not made love to her because he had not respected her. Was he now regretting that decision? And suddenly Suki knew a way to hit back. 'And what if I have?' she asked softly, deliberately letting a small, secret smile hover around the edges of her lips.

He stilled as though he'd been struck, the brief flare of fury in his dark eyes making him seem like some modern-day incarnation of the devil. Then he nodded. 'I was a fool,' he ground out, 'not to have had you when you were mine for the taking! Not to have taken you over and over again, so that you would never forget me. To imprint myself on your body and on your mind— so that whenever you lay with another man it would be *me* you thought of, *me* you tasted, *me* you longed to have in your arms, *me* filling your body, making you sob with pleasure.'

The savage sexual boast had precisely the wrong effect on her. It started that awful aching; it unleashed that nebulous emotion which only he had ever inspired, the one she had once mistakenly thought was love, but now, with hindsight, realised had been nothing more than an overpoweringly primitive need to be possessed by him which at the time she had not been able to control.

And now?

Was it possible that she was still prey to the same appalling needs, an identical hunger which he could somehow provoke with just one hot, dark look?

Her lids fluttered to shade the confused and feverish glittering in her amber eyes. 'Please go,' she told him from between parched lips, afraid even to look at him, for fear that he should be able to read her longing and her confusion with the uncanny perception he had once had in such abundance where she was concerned.

'Go?' he echoed softly, and Suki jumped, startled, to find that he had moved soundlessly across the carpet and was now beside her, was staring down at her, so close that she could feel his breath fanning her cheek.

'Yes, go,' she whispered, wondering what dark magic he could weave just by being there.

She could hear the smile in his voice as he spoke. 'But you don't want me to go, do you, *cara*?'

'Yes.' But she lied. She wanted only one thing and that was to taste his lips on hers again, and she closed her eyes and unconsciously swayed towards him.

No!

Her eyes snapped open in horror at what she had almost let happen, but she was frozen by the astounded look of disbelief she saw on Pasquale's face—as though he too was gripped in the power of something far stronger than reason.

He pulled her unprotesting into his arms then and stared down at her face. 'Exquisite,' he murmured softly as his gaze slowly and deliberately raked over her dazed face to where her eyes glittered like amber jewels. 'Utterly exquisite. And just begging to be kissed.'

'No,' she whimpered even as she looked with longing at the lips poised just inches away.

'Oh, yes, Suki,' he contradicted. '*Yes.*'

But the kiss was not the brutal and punishing onslaught she was expecting. It was tender and evocative—and it hinted at something she had been searching for all her life. She heard him make some small, indistinct sound as her lips opened beneath his, and as if from a long way off came the sound of her own voice, echoing his sigh as his tongue moved inside her mouth to deepen the kiss.

Suki was lost, his sweet, sweet kiss sucking her into the irresistible vortex of desire. She felt it flooding her veins with wild power, to centralise into a flickering flame which slowly began to unfurl in the pit of her stomach. She tried to stop him, just once, but it was a pathetic little effort, and the two hands which had started to push ineffectually at his shoulders somehow instead became entwined at the back of his strong neck, her fingers fluttering helplessly into the luxuriant black hair which grew there.

His hands moved to her hips, and he ran them deliberately down over the slender curves before sliding them beneath her buttocks and lifting her quite effortlessly to carry her over to the bed and tumble them both down on top of it.

And even after that bold declaration of intent she did nothing to stop him. Her breathing was erratic, her thought processes gone haywire as she stared at him with hungry, confused eyes. 'Pasquale...' she managed. 'Don't do this. Please.'

There was no softening of the implacable line
of his mouth as he traced a finger from neck to
breast and she shivered in helpless response. 'But
you want me, *cara*. Quite as much as I want you.
Don't you? *Don't you?*'

Wordlessly, she shook her head.

'Yes. You do. So why stop when we both know
how very good it will be?'

He moved his arm up the pillow to smooth her
hair back from her face, but Suki could have
sworn that his gaze flickered to the wristwatch
which gleamed gold against his olive skin. That
odd movement jarred, and was enough to make
her begin to pull free from the tempting circle of
his arms, when suddenly there was a light rap on
the door.

'Hi, Suki,' called a cheerful voice. 'Are you
decent? I got your message!' And the door
opened to reveal Salvatore standing there, his face
rigid with shock as he took in the sight of Suki
lying tangled in Pasquale's arms on the bed.

'Dear God!' he exclaimed, and his face went
white. 'Pasquale!'

Pasquale gave a lazy smile. 'Yes?'

Salvatore swallowed. 'What the hell are you
doing here?'

'I'm making love to a woman—what does it
look like? And you happen to be disturbing us.'

'But I—'

Pasquale's eyes were like steel traps. 'Get out,
Salvatore—before I'm tempted to punch you. In
this instance, I'm happy to take your place to
keep the lady happy—but I'm warning you that

if you ever think of straying again, then wherever you are I'll come and find you and tear every limb from your body. Is that understood?'

Salvatore swallowed with fear, and Suki couldn't blame him. She struggled free, an acrid taste in her mouth, feeling as though she was in the middle of some bizarre dream as she stumbled off the bed. 'What the hell is going on?' she demanded.

'Salvatore is just leaving,' came the grim voice. 'Aren't you?'

Salvatore nodded, swallowing convulsively, before backing towards the door.

Fragments of conversation came fluttering back to Suki as she moved as far away from the bed as possible, while he continued to lie there, a mocking look of amusement on his face as he watched her.

'Message?' she said aloud, frowning as she spoke. 'Salvatore said that he'd received a message—but I sent him no message.'

He gave a low laugh. 'No, indeed, but he spoke the truth—I left a message with one of the waitresses that he should come to your room in half an hour. That was the amount of time I estimated it would take for me to have you in my arms.' He glanced briefly at his watch with a sardonic smile. 'But it seems that my estimation was conservative, since I managed to accomplish it in just twenty minutes.' He sighed. 'Always so responsive, *bella mia*.'

The knowledge that he was right did little to soothe Suki's temper, and a red mist of fury swam before her eyes. She lifted the heavy silver-backed hairbrush from the dressing table and hurled it at him without thinking of the consequences, but he caught it in mid-air with the confidence of a county-class cricket player.

'Naughty!' he murmured, and casually got up from the bed as though she hadn't been scrabbling around like a madwoman for further missiles to launch at him.

A shoe, a coat-hanger, a full handbag... Humiliatingly he caught them all and tossed them onto the bed, still with that contemptuous half-smile on his mouth.

Out of breath now, hurt and bewildered, Suki stared at him. 'Why?' she asked him. 'Just tell me why.'

'Why what?' he queried softly.

'Why you tricked him into coming here, and let him see us... us...'

'On the verge of making love?' he prompted helpfully.

Colour rushed in to stain her cheeks. 'No, we weren't,' she mumbled.

'Liar!' he taunted softly.

Did he have a better nature for her to appeal to? She turned to him. 'Why couldn't you have just settled for telling me to lay off? That he was engaged to Cristina? Surely you know that I would never have anything to do with a man who was engaged to someone else?'

He shrugged. 'That's just the problem; I know very little about you, Suki—other than the fact that you have an extraordinary physical appeal, which actually has me in its thrall too.' A note of puzzlement came into his voice and his eyes hardened into slivers of jet. 'Which is extraordinary in itself, since I am not usually attracted to women I dislike.

'And, since you ask, the reason I did not simply ask either you or Salvatore to "lay off", as you so inelegantly expressed it, and leave it at that is because I am a man who leaves nothing to chance. I could not guarantee that you would heed my request, and, yes, I could have threatened Salvatore into leaving you alone, but I preferred him to witness with his own eyes just what kind of woman he had chosen to have his affair with: the kind of woman who would deceive him with another man at the first opportunity which arose. Why should I expect him to take *my* word for it, when firsthand experience would doubtless be so much more effective?

'Take my word for it, *cara*—Salvatore shall not stray again. And the very qualities which make you such ideal mistress material will reinforce Cristina's suitability as a wife.'

For a moment, Suki was stunned into speechlessness as she stared back into those cold, mocking eyes. But not for long. 'My God,' she breathed in disbelief. 'You cold-hearted, manipulative *bastard*! Get out! Get out of here before I scream the house down.'

He nodded, looking as though this time he was about to accede to her demand. 'Certainly. Doubtless you wish to change.' His eyes briefly flicked over her body, and Suki remembered that she was wearing nothing but her bikini covered by a wholly inadequate silk wrap. 'But before I do I have a proposition to put to you which you may find interesting.'

Suki's mouth tightened. '*Nothing* you could say would ever be remotely interesting to me!'

'Don't be melodramatic, Suki. Never turn an offer down before you've even heard it. I'm giving you the opportunity of a lifetime—'

'The promise that I'll never have the misfortune to set eyes on your conniving face again?' she hazarded acidly.

'On the contrary,' he said, in a voice as smooth as honey. 'I want you to become my mistress.'

There was a stunned silence as Suki stared across the room at Pasquale with growing horror. 'I don't believe you just said that,' she said eventually, her voice rising with incredulity. 'You must be completely mad!'

His dark eyes glittered as he acknowledged her remark. 'Perhaps just a little,' he murmured. 'But that is the effect you seem to have on me.'

'Either that or you've got a very warped sense of humour.'

'No. I never, ever joke about business,' he said as coolly as if he had this kind of bizarre conversation every day.

'*Business?* You define your ludicrous and insulting proposition as *business*?'

'But of course. That is what being a mistress is about, is it not? An exchange of commodities. You would have all the many advantages of being my lover. As well as the obvious pleasure, there

would be all the baubles and the luxury trips,
and in return I would possess that exquisitely
beautiful body.'

He frowned at her expression. 'Oh, come,
come, Suki; please don't insult me by fixing me
with that shocked look, as though you've just
left the convent. You must have been propositioned many times before. Very recently, too. Or
are you telling me that you would have gone off
for a weekend with Salvatore if the destination
had been a grimy, industrial town somewhere instead of a luxury villa in the Mediterranean?
Admit it, why don't you—that like most women
you are dazzled by the accoutrements of wealth?'

What a cynic! she thought in disbelief. Suki's
voice was very soft as she looked at him with real
loathing, her amber eyes sparking as if they were
lit from behind with fire, and said, 'I don't intend
to justify my behaviour to you—quite frankly,
your mind is so warped I doubt that whatever I
said would make any difference.

'But I will tell you one thing, Pasquale—that
if you were the last man on earth I still wouldn't
consent to be your mistress—and that's no idle
promise! You see, for one thing I earn enough
money to buy my *own* baubles, and finance my
*own* trips. I'm an independent woman and I never
have and I never *will* be bought off by some
man!'

She glowered at him, quite out of breath after
her passionate response. 'But even more importantly,' she continued, once she'd got her breath
back, 'mistresses, like all women, require more

than baubles and luxury trips—even the most hard-hearted of them require some modicum of affection and respect. But those don't seem to be words which figure in your vocabulary—perhaps they never did. You seem to be incapable of either. Anyway—' she glared at him '—I don't wish to discuss it any further. So go.'

'And I gather I am to take that as a refusal?' he mocked, then gave a sexy, sardonic smile. 'Such fighting words, Suki, and I respond to nothing better than a challenge!'

If only his voice didn't sound so rich and velvety and downright irresistible, Suki thought resentfully. 'Take it as a permanent refusal, Pasquale—I would so *hate* you to get your hopes up,' she finished with a sarcasm which he seemed to find amusing. 'Now are you going?'

'Yes, I'm going.' He spoke with quiet emphasis as his hand curved over the shiny brass of the doorhandle. 'But we shall see,' he threatened, on a silky note. 'We shall see just how "permanent" a refusal it is. I am a determined man. Believe me when I tell you, Suki, that I want you more than I've ever wanted *any* woman, and, what is more, I intend to have you. Seven years ago we started something that I want to see finished,' he concluded on a husky note, and the door closed softly behind him before a shocked Suki could even begin to formulate an answer.

Ten minutes after he had left her room there was another tap on the door, which a dazed Suki scarcely heard. She was sitting on the edge of the bed, deciding that Pasquale's bizarre invitation to become his mistress, and his talk of responding to a challenge, had merely been made in a mad moment of sexual frustration. And that there was absolutely no reason why she ever need see him again.

The tapping resumed.

'Go away!' she yelled automatically.

'Suki! I must talk to you! Please! It's important!'

It was Salvatore's voice, and Suki stormed over to the door and flung it open.

'Why the hell didn't you tell me you were engaged to Pasquale Caliandro's secretary?' she demanded. 'In fact, why the hell didn't you tell me you were engaged—full stop?'

'But it was all perfectly legit—a working weekend,' said Salvatore plaintively. 'We weren't *doing* anything to be ashamed of!'

'Too right we weren't, but that isn't how it must look to Pasquale, the interfering tyrant.'

Salvatore looked anxiously up and down the corridor, as if he was expecting the man himself to suddenly materialise. 'Someone might hear you—can't I come in?'

'No, you can't come in! Are you out of your mind? If you value your health I'd recommend staying away from me, and any other woman as well—apart from Cristina. Pasquale isn't the kind of man to give you more than one chance. So if you really *do* want to marry Cristina I'd strongly recommend that you adopt the masculine equivalent of purdah!'

He held the palms of his hands up in appeal. 'Suki, please let me come inside and I can explain everything—but what I *don't* want is for Pasquale to see me here.'

'Why not?'

'Because he terrifies the life out of me,' Salvatore admitted ruefully.

'Then you probably have more sense than I gave you credit for,' said Suki grimly, and opened the door wider. 'OK, you can come in. And I'm giving you five minutes to explain. *Everything!*'

Salvatore sighed. 'It's difficult.'

Suki looked at him questioningly. 'Just what did you tell your fiancée about this trip? Why was she crying down the phone to Pasquale?'

He licked his lips nervously. 'Er—that's just it—I didn't. Tell her anything, that is. Or rather I told her that I was doing a shoot. I just didn't tell her that it was with you.'

'And why not?'

He shrugged apologetically. 'She gets—er—you know—very jealous.'

Suki's eyes narrowed disbelievingly. 'Oh, come on, Salvatore! You're surely not expecting me to believe *that*? As a photographer, you work with models all the time! If she was jealous then the relationship wouldn't last a minute.'

'It isn't other models,' he told her, with an embarrassed look. 'Just you.'

Suki's eyes glittered dangerously. 'I think you'd better explain what you mean, don't you?'

He shrugged again helplessly. Suddenly, for all his photographic genius, he looked terribly, terribly young. 'Just that she knows that I've always been desperate to take your photo. And when I first met her I had a bit of a thing about you. I even—er—had a poster of you on my bedroom wall.' He blushed.

Suki closed her eyes briefly and then gave a slightly hysterical laugh. 'If only you knew how old that makes me feel,' she said wearily. 'Didn't it occur to you that she'd find out some time and that she would react in precisely this way?'

He shook his head. 'I didn't really think at all,' he admitted. 'I was so keen to photograph you, and I couldn't believe it when you said yes. I'm sorry, Suki.'

Suki sighed. How had she managed to do it again? Now there was a fiancée on the war-path, for absolutely no reason. Was she just too trusting? Or simply a fool? 'You'd better go back to New York and make your peace with her,' she told him. 'No doubt your friends can vouch that we've been given separate rooms, but for goodness' sake you'd better leave now.'

'And what will you do?' he asked her anxiously.

'Me? I'm on the first plane out of here,' said Suki grimly. And with a bit of luck I can put this whole ghastly incident out of my mind, she added silently.

And when the door had closed behind Salvatore Suki strode over to the wardrobe and, without bothering to fold anything, swept all her clothes out and began piling them into her suitcase.

# CHAPTER FOUR

SUKI unlocked the front door of her London flat and slammed it shut behind her, dropping her suitcase in the hall and hurrying along the corridor to turn the central heating on.

Brr! Her fingers fumbled with the dial.

How great to be home, she thought appreciatively as she kicked off her shoes and padded through into the sitting room whose bright crimson walls were almost completely covered with her own paintings.

She had flown into Heathrow from Nice to be greeted with absolutely *foul* weather—just the kind of thing you expected in England in the middle of summer! It was grey, windy and rainy.

And it matched her mood exactly!

She had upgraded her air ticket to first-class for the flight home, and consequently had had enough leg room to sleep for the short flight home, but, typically, had been unable to catch even a wink. And now she was exhausted. Absolutely exhausted. Which wasn't that surprising when she thought about it. Apart from the emotional stress of seeing Pasquale again, she was suffering from the effects of jet lag.

Still, at least she had managed to sneak away from the villa without bumping into Pasquale. She must be grateful for small mercies.

The red light on her Ansaphone was flashing. Just two messages—but then she *did* guard her telephone number as though it were Fort Knox!

Suki punched the button. The first call was from her brother. His voice sounded strained, but then these days it always seemed to sound strained.

'Hello, Suki; I need to talk to you urgently. Can you ring me at the office—*not* at home? I don't want Kirstie worrying.'

Suki sighed. It couldn't be *another* request for money to bail him out, surely? She'd only just injected some funds into the ailing family business. At least when their mother had been alive she had managed to exercise a little restraint over Piers's expensive tastes. But lately the requests for money had been getting more and more frequent. Piers had taken several foolish risks on the stock market which hadn't come off, and although his wife, Kirstie, was a dear, Suki privately thought that she let Piers get away with murder.

If *I* were married to him, I wouldn't let him fritter it all away, she thought grimly. But their son, Toby, was almost two years old, and Suki doted on her adorable little nephew. And it was concern for *his* welfare more than anything else which made it impossible for her to refuse any of Piers's requests for funds.

She immediately picked up the receiver and dialled Piers's office, to be told that he wasn't back from lunch yet.

Suki glanced at her watch. At *four o'clock*? 'Will you please tell him that his sister called?' she said to his secretary. 'And I'll be at home.' No wonder the business was doing badly if its managing director spent the whole afternoon closeted in a restaurant, she thought crossly as she replaced the receiver.

The second message was from Carly, her agent, and the confident American accent rang out.

'Hi, honey. I know you're in France, but ring me just as *soon* as you get back. Something's come up and, believe me, it's a once-in-a-lifetime! So *ring* me!'

Suki was contemplating doing just that when the phone rang.

It was Carly again.

'You're back! Thank heavens!' she exclaimed.

'I just got in.'

'Good time?'

Pasquale's face loomed darkly in her mind, despite all her vows not to give him another thought. 'In a word—no.'

'What happened?'

Pasquale Caliandro, that's what happened, she thought grimly. 'Salvatore Bruni, the photographer,' said Suki grimly, 'neglected to tell me that he has a pathologically jealous fiancée, who sent a knight in shining armour—' now *why* had she automatically given Pasquale such a romantic association? '—to warn me off,' she finished lamely.

'Oh, dear!' laughed Carly. 'Never mind—I have just the thing to cheer you up.'

'What? A one-way ticket to the moon?'

Carly laughed again. 'Come on, Suki—it's not like you to be negative; after all, this isn't the first time this kind of thing has happened.'

'Exactly. I'm thinking of having my head shaved and going into a monastery—'

'Nunnery.'

'Whatever,' quipped Suki, thinking that a male-free zone seemed like a more attractive prospect by the minute.

'Well, before you do you'd better hear what it is I've got to say. Can I come round?'

'When?'

'Now! It's rather important.'

Half an hour later Carly was in Suki's sitting room, dunking a rosehip and wild cherry teabag into a mug of boiling water.

'Yuk!' shuddered Suki as she sipped her hot chocolate. 'I don't know how you can touch that stuff!'

'It helps me stay thin.' Carly eyed Suki's mug reprovingly. 'Did I ever tell you that your metabolism is grossly unfair?'

'Constantly.' Suki smiled. 'Now what did you want to see me about?'

Carly beamed. 'How would earning five million bucks in the next five years grab you?'

Suki pulled a face. 'Yes, I know—and the moon is made out of green cheese! Come on, Carly, I'm too tired for jokes.'

Carly shook her head, her shrewd blue eyes sparking with excitement. 'It's your lucky day, honey—I know that much.' She took a deep breath. 'Formidable. Heard of them?'

'Of course I've heard of them. They're one of the biggest make-up and perfumery companies in the world, aren't they?'

'Second biggest—but they're aiming for the top. And they're offering you a contract over the next five years. They want you to become the new Formidable girl. The offer only came in over the weekend; I still can't believe it!'

Suki just stared at her agent as her mind tried to take in this astonishing news. 'Work for Formidable?' she asked slowly.

'You've got it in one, honey!'

'On an exclusive contract?'

Carly shrugged. 'Sure. That's the way these things go—the company won't want you advertising for anyone else. When the public see your face, they think Formidable. But the money's *fantastic*—and I've had my lawyer take a look at the contract.' She paused. 'He was impressed. *Very* impressed.'

Which really *was* saying something. Carly's lawyer should have had 'CYNIC' emblazoned across his forehead!

Suki shook her head in bemusement. Exclusive contracts were few and far between. 'But why me?' she wanted to know.

Carly sipped at her tea. 'They've just been taken over by some hot-shot who apparently saw you in last year's suncream commercial. So either he likes redheads or he's a sucker for tall women!'

It took Suki about five seconds to think it over. She thought of the lecherous photographer in New York. She thought of Piers and the constant drain he was on her resources. She thought about getting older, of having to compete on the catwalk with models of sixteen. Of desperately searching in the mirror for the lines on her face which would signify the beginning of the end.

She drained the last of her hot chocolate and put the cup down. 'When do I sign?' she asked.

Carly gave a satisfied smile. 'How about Monday?'

'If you could just sign both copies of the contract, Miss Franklin. That is, if you're satisfied with the contents, of course.'

Suki took the pen from the Formidable lawyer, who had spent the last half-hour gazing at her like a moonstruck schoolboy. They were sitting round the glossy round table in the vast boardroom of Formidable's impressive London headquarters. 'On the dotted line, I presume?' she queried, hoping that she sounded efficient, and not like someone to whom legal jargon was about as understandable as hieroglyphics!

'The very same!' he said admiringly.

Suki couldn't help feeling a little fizz of excitement as she signed her name with a flourish.

'I do hope you realise that you've just signed your life away!' said the Formidable lawyer jovially.

'Rubbish!' laughed Suki as she put the top back on her fountain pen. 'My lawyer has been through it with a fine-tooth comb.'

'I've never known a deal go through so *quickly*,' said Carly admiringly, an irrepressible smile hovering around her lips. Probably thinking of her ten per cent, thought Suki wryly.

The lawyer ran his hand back through his elegant silver hair. 'That's our new owner for you,' he murmured, directing his attention entirely towards Suki. 'A man not noted for letting the grass grow beneath his feet.'

'Anyone I know?' asked Carly immediately, her antennae out, her curiosity roused.

The lawyer gave a discreet shake of his head. 'I'm not at liberty to discuss that. He's a man who prefers to make his own introductions.' He glanced down at his watch. 'But he'll be here at any minute to do just that. Ah!' And he stood up as the door of the boardroom opened.

The frightening thing was that Suki *knew*. Whether or not it was just some sixth sense she had in connection with the man, she couldn't have said, but Suki actually knew in the few moments before she turned round and stared into those dark, mocking eyes just who it was who was now the new owner of Formidable.

Outraged, she sprang to her feet as she stared across the room in horror at Pasquale's infuriatingly handsome face. *'You!'* she accused. 'You cheating, underhand, manipulative—!'

'Suki!' mouthed Carly in horror.

'Miss Franklin, *please*,' begged the silver-haired lawyer, who couldn't have looked more shocked at her outburst if he'd just seen an apparition.

Suki ignored both of them. 'You think that you can go through life getting your own way all the time, don't you? Well, you're wrong! *Wrong!* Completely and utterly wrong! Just because I didn't fall down at your feet and agree to become your... your... *mistress*, you actually have the blatant nerve to think that you can *buy* me! Well, you can't, Pasquale—and what's more I'll prove it to you!'

And, so saying, Suki picked up the contract nearest to her and deliberately ripped it into tiny shreds which fluttered down like snowflakes onto the thick cream carpet.

Like two people hypnotised, Carly and the lawyer just sat in stunned silence and watched, while, to Suki's outrage, Pasquale's reaction was the last in the world she would have anticipated. She had expected him to be absolutely furious that she had announced his nefarious designs to all and sundry, but to her astonishment he was laughing. Actually *laughing!* With the corners of that too delectable mouth quirking upwards in a smile which was quite devastating in its impact.

'Bravo, *bella*!' he applauded softly. 'Bravo! Truly an inspiring performance!'

The silver-haired lawyer had hastily grabbed the remaining contract and was holding it protectively against his chest like a shield. 'Miss Franklin!' he admonished sternly. 'I have to tell you that you are in breach of contract. And that I am afraid you give me no option other than to—'

'Leave us,' Pasquale interjected smoothly.

The lawyer fixed him with an astonished stare. 'But Signor Caliandro. . .' he began.

But Pasquale was shaking his head. 'I said leave us,' he said emphatically.

Suki was still so angry that she was literally shaking. 'Good!' she stormed wildly. 'I'm glad if I've broken the contract! It's no longer worth the paper it's written on!'

Carly shuddered as she stared in horror at the scraps of contract which littered the thick carpet. 'Suki, honey,' she hissed, 'I don't know what all this is about, but please, *please*—just don't say any more. I beg you.'

Pasquale indicated the door with an impatient shake of his head. 'If you would leave us now.'

Carly and the lawyer reluctantly trooped out of the boardroom like children ordered outside into the garden to play and Suki sent a hot, angry glare at Pasquale.

'So how's the great controller?' she asked sarcastically. 'Have you managed to sort out your secretary's love-life?'

'I have advised Salvatore to bring the wedding forward,' he said blandly as he held out the nearest chair for her. 'Please sit down.'

He had done this, and he had the *nerve* to ask her to sit down? 'I won't be here long enough to sit down.' Just long enough to give the arrogant manipulator a piece of her mind!

'As you wish.' He sat down on the edge of the Camelot-sized table, spreading his long legs out in front of him and regarding her with interest from beneath the dark, hooded eyes as if waiting to see what she would do next, and Suki met his cool gaze with a steady stare, her mind and her eyes working separately as one tried to deny what the other reluctantly admitted.

That he looked an absolute knockout.

He was dressed for work. The suit he wore was everything she liked on a man but so rarely saw. No man had the right to look that good in a suit. In beautifully cut grey linen, it merely hinted at the muscular strength which lay beneath, and yet in a peculiar way that emphasised his fabulous physique far more than if he'd been wearing something clinging. He wore with it a wonderful pale blue silk shirt and a dark blue silk tie knotted at his throat. The outfit was wildly expensive, yet beautifully understated. Pasquale had, she acknowledged, a style all his own.

She could see that he was subjecting her to his own cool appraisal and she was glad that the circumstances which had led to her being here meant that she'd dressed in her most businesslike outfit. Not that she *felt* in the least bit businesslike at the moment—especially not with those dark eyes glittering at her—but she certainly looked the part.

Her slub-silk suit, with its short skirt and boxy jacket, was in a vivid shade of purple, contrasting flatteringly with the pale auburn of her hair which today she wore knotted back into a sophisticated chignon. Beneath the suit she wore a cream body. Her long legs were encased in pale stockings and her purple, high-heeled suede shoes matched the suit exactly. In these shoes she towered over most men, but not, infuriatingly, over *this* man.

This man towered over *her*.

He gave a slow smile. 'Yes,' he said finally. 'I like the way you look. I like it very much...' His voice tailed off on a suggestive murmur, and Suki was shocked to feel her body respond to that murmur in spite of her anger, her nipples hardening beneath the silky rub of the body. What had he done to her all those years ago? Imprinted and dominated and stamped himself on her psyche to such a degree that he, and only he, could make her melt beneath that dark gaze?

'I'm not looking for your approval,' she told him, shaken by her physical response to him. 'And I can tell you now that I won't work for you.'

'But you wouldn't be working for me, not directly.' He gave her a cool look and his voice sounded almost reasonable.

Snake!

'After all, it isn't as though I'm asking you to sit in the typing pool, now is it?' he added smoothly.

Suki almost spluttered with indignation. 'Directly or indirectly, the answer's the same. I won't do it! And you can't make me!'

'Oh, can't I?' he queried silkily, surveying her from beneath the hooded flare of his eyes until she could bear it no longer.

'Why me?' she demanded. 'Are there no lengths you won't go to to get your own way? I simply can't believe that you would actually hire me—at vast expense—to be your in-house model, just to...to...'

'To?' he interrogated coolly, but there was a spark of amusement in the dark eyes.

'To make me your mistress!' she declared.

He gave a faint smile. 'You do me a dishonour, *cara*,' he murmured. 'I am first and foremost a businessman.'

Business. There was that wretched word again. The one he'd used about mistresses, too. 'Oh, really?' she mocked.

'Yes. *Really*.' He looked at the stubborn set of her jaw. 'What would you say if I told you that you had been selected to be the Formidable woman because you have the looks, the charisma and the image we're looking for to portray our products perfectly?'

'I'd say you were lying out of the back of your teeth! There are *thousands* of models you could have chosen.'

'But unfortunately, *bella mia*, none that look quite like you,' he said, very softly, his eyes narrowing as they appraised her, and she had to steel herself not to tremble at the seductive undertones in his voice and that frankly gorgeous stare. Suki drew in a deep breath preparatory to flouncing out, but he stayed her with his next words.

'My lawyer is perfectly correct, you know,' he observed quietly. 'If I choose to sue you, you don't have a leg to stand on. Metaphorically speaking, I could take you to the cleaners, Suki.'

'And I don't care!' she answered defiantly. 'Sue me! Take every penny I've got! Poverty would be an attractive alternative to working for you!'

To her fury, he laughed again, showing teeth which looked brilliantly white against the olive of his skin. 'I see that over the years you have developed a magnificent fighting spirit. And a proud, stubborn streak. That is good—I like a woman with backbone.'

'What did you expect? That I'd be the same young and naïve, docile little girl who—?' She broke off, her cheeks flushing scarlet as she realised what she had been about to say.

'Begged me to make love to her?' he interjected in a silky voice. 'For one so young and so naïve—as you claim—you certainly knew how to give voice to your desires.'

She stared at him, her cheeks hot, her heart racing. 'Will you never let me forget that?' she whispered.

He shook his head. 'How can I, *cara*, when I cannot forget it myself?' he declared simply.

Something in his voice sounded softer than mere desire, and Suki found herself reacting to it as a starving dog would leap on a scrap of meat. She became aware that her nipples were peaking painfully, hidden by the looseness of her jacket.

It was as if her body was no longer hers, no longer governed by the self-control she was determined to fix on it. And Pasquale was responsible for this frightening loss of control.

He was dangerous. He always had been dangerous. At seventeen she had found him irresistible. Seven years on it was disturbing to discover that his appeal had only become magnified. She could not fight him, not effectively—which left her with only one alternative.

To run.

She swallowed the lump in her throat. 'I think I've made myself clear,' she told him. 'So there's really nothing more to say.'

'Suki,' he told her softly, 'I don't think you quite realise your position.'

She looked him straight in the eye, the stubborn pride he'd spoken of blazing from her face. 'Oh, I think I do, Pasquale. I'm no fool. Sue me, and I'll take the consequences. I mean it.'

'So I see.' He frowned, then spoke his next words almost reluctantly. 'Do you realise that your brother is on the verge of bankruptcy?'

Something in the tone of his voice sent a frisson of fear skating down her spine. Piers? 'Of course he isn't,' she said calmly, though her heart was hammering in her chest like a piston.

'I'm afraid he is.'

There was a confidence about the way he spoke, a certainty, which chilled her. 'How on earth can you know about Piers's financial situation?' she said. 'You haven't gone and bought *his* company, have you?' she finished sarcastically.

He acknowledged the jibe with a nod of his dark head. 'I don't take on losing ventures.'

'Everyone has been hit by the recession,' said Suki defensively. 'But the end is in sight; everyone says so.'

'And that,' he answered sardonically, 'is certainly true in your brother's case.'

Suki somehow knew that he wasn't lying to her, and yet still she sought to deny it. She shook her head and a strand of auburn hair came loose. 'He can't be. He can't. I gave—' She clamped her mouth tightly shut, aware of what she had been about to say.

'Yes, *cara*?'

'Nothing.'

'You gave him—money?'

Suki held onto her purple clutch-bag as though it were a lifeline. 'That's between my brother and me—'

'*No!*' And he stood up from the table, his face dark and suddenly furious. 'It isn't just between you and your brother. There are other people involved, Suki. There are the shareholders, for one thing—people who have a right to know that their investment is safe, not being squandered away by some spoilt boy who cannot or will not accept that his endeavours simply won't support the kind of lifestyle he has become used to!'

His quick glance took in her white face, but he carried on regardless. 'He also has a wife and a very young child, does he not? What right does your brother have to jeopardise their very livelihood?'

Suki sat down suddenly, her legs buckling beneath her, and Pasquale immediately reached over to the centre of the table and poured her a glass of mineral water.

'Here,' he said abruptly.

She took the glass and drank from it, her long eyelashes fluttering to shield her eyes as she shakily replaced the glass on the table. When she raised her eyes to him again her voice sounded miraculously calm. 'What do you want?'

He nodded, satisfied now that he had her capitulation. 'I want you to stop dishing out money to your brother, for a start. Though that in itself is now becoming academic, since your funds wouldn't even make a small dent in the kind of debts he is in the process of building up. But even if you carry on supporting him in the smallest way, then you're simply helping him to deny that there's a problem. And unless he admits that there *is* a problem, then there is little hope for him in the future. With your assistance, he'll never be prepared to change.'

Suki tried and failed to imagine Piers ever changing. 'And what if he refuses to change?'

Pasquale's mouth was a thin line. 'He doesn't have any alternative. In a few days the banks will foreclose on the loans he's taken out.'

'Then it's too late anyway!' said Suki wildly.

He shook his head. 'Not if I buy into the company—make sure that the loans are paid.'

Suki frowned. 'But you said—'

'I said *what, bella mia*?' he asked, in a voice of velvet and silk.

'That you—you never take on losing ventures.'

'Bravo!' he applauded softly. 'So she listens, too. A woman who listens is a rare prize!'

She really wasn't in any kind of position to point out his chauvinism, and, what was more, her heart was thudding as the realisation of just how trapped she was slowly began to dawn on her.

'But I am prepared to make an exception in this case,' he told her, with a flash of his dark eyes. 'Besides, under my guidance Franklin Motors will undergo a dramatic change of fortunes; it will assume greatness once again.'

'And then what?' she asked him shakily. 'You sack Piers?'

'Sack him? You think I am such a hard man?'

'Yes, I do.'

He laughed. 'I do not intend to sack him, *cara*, no. As I told you, under my guidance we will get the company up and running.'

'Oh? Have you suddenly become an expert on car manufacturing?' she asked sarcastically.

He smiled. 'I am an expert on manufacturing in general,' he said. 'The specifics can easily be adapted to the theory—that supply should never outstrip demand. I am also an expert in predicting trends, and currently there is a demand for the small, specialist sports car for which the Franklin firm rightly became so famous. Your brother's error was in overexpanding and trying to compete in the mass market, but that is easily remedied.'

Suki digested this. Unfortunately, he was right—damn him! He was doing nothing more than succinctly voicing the vague fears she'd had for ages. How very galling! She met the speculative look in his eyes. 'And I suppose you're an expert on women, too, are you?' she heard herself saying.

A sardonic dark eyebrow was raised. 'Let's just say that any expertise I may lay claim to in that *particular* field has never been questioned.' He gave her a mocking glance. 'But maybe that's all about to change, Suki.'

Her heart pounded. What did he mean by that? 'So you're going to buy into Piers's company? That's very—kind—of you, Pasquale.'

He gave her a strange look. 'Kind? I do not do it out of kindness, *cara*, but I think you know that. Call it a favour, if you like.'

'And in return for this—favour?'

'That too I think you know.'

His eyes told her what he wanted in return— *her*! But she wasn't going to let him wriggle out of saying it, admitting it. Let him acknowledge aloud the depths to which he was prepared to sink to to get her into his bed—the barbaric swine! 'No,' she said flatly. 'I'm not sure that I do. Why don't you tell me, Pasquale?'

He smiled, but it was a cold smile, totally lacking in humour. 'It's simple. Be the Formidable girl.'

That completely took the wind out of her sails. 'You mean just that?' she queried incredulously. 'You mean you don't want—' she blurted out, before pulling herself up short.

'Mmm?' he prompted softly.

She held her chin up. 'That's all?' she asked proudly.

He shook his head, and his eyes glittered with terrifying promise. 'No, it is not all, but it will do for now. I have stated my claim and my desire for you to become my mistress. And I can wait, Suki, but not for long. Believe me when I tell you that I am not a patient man.'

She gave him a long, steady look as she acknowledged his outrageous audacity in talking about it so coolly. Clearly not a man who was governed by the normal social niceties! 'And how far do you propose to go to get what you want— namely me?'

He seemed momentarily surprised by *her* frankness, for his dark eyes glittered briefly as he met her stare full-on. 'I'm not sure I understand exactly what you mean, *cara*,' he said softly.

'I want to know whether force is one of your less charming characteristics,' she said brutally, pleased when she saw his mouth harden with displeasure.

'Force?' he echoed. 'I think you know in your heart that it is not, Suki. I never take anything from a woman that she is not prepared to give.'

And his eyes issued her a mocking challenge which she did not dare to answer.

## CHAPTER FIVE

PASQUALE indubitably had the upper hand, Suki realised as she stared up into the steely glint of his eyes, and there wasn't a damned thing she could do about it. 'And if I accept this bizarre offer to work for your company—'

'You really have no choice,' he interrupted smoothly, shaking his dark head. 'Do you?'

No. That was just it. She didn't.

He was right. Again. That was the most infuriating thing. She really *couldn't* keep on pouring cash into Piers's company while he carried on squandering it. Quite apart from the fact—as Pasquale himself had infuriatingly pointed out—that Piers's debts were far outstripping her capital.

And if she refused to become the Formidable girl, then not only would Franklin Motors be ruined but Pasquale could still rightly sue her for breach of contract. He could ruin her financially. He could label her as unreliable. He could see that she never worked again. She had to face it, she thought wearily—whichever way she turned, he had her—she was trapped.

'Let me get something straight,' she said slowly.

'I'm listening.'

'The deal is that I work for you—nothing more than that?'

He lifted both elegant shoulders in a very Continental shrug. 'As I said before—nothing more than you wish to give.'

'And what are the terms of employment?'

'The terms will remain the same as those in the contract you signed,' he said, his mouth twisting into a deprecating half-smile as he surveyed the fragments of contract which still littered the carpet. 'And you had no problems with that until you knew that I was behind it, did you?'

'No,' she replied reluctantly. 'And when do I start?' she asked, realising that the question had effectively sealed her fate, a fact which did not escape him either, for he gave a bland smile.

'There will be a party at the Granchester Hotel tomorrow evening to introduce you to the international press. A car will be sent for you at eight.'

Smoothing her short skirt down, Suki rose to her feet. 'And just what image am I to project as the Formidable girl?' she queried.

He smiled. An exciting smile this time. A predatory smile. It made her shiver. It made her thrill. It made her want to rake her nails down the side of that delectable face. It made her want to kiss him.

'Well, certainly not one of innocence,' he said cruelly. 'You will be the embodiment of glamour, *bella mia*. And sex appeal,' he added, his eyes straying from her face to her body in a lazy stare.

Suki suppressed another small shudder. Surely she should feel affronted when he looked at her like that? Surely she shouldn't experience that aching little frisson of excitement?

'A stylist from the advertising agency will be around at seven with a complete outfit for you to wear. We use Lomas & Lomas,' he finished. And then, quite without warning, he reached down and caught her hand, moving it slowly to his lips, his eyes never leaving her face, capturing her reluctantly, enthralling her. 'I am very happy, *cara*, that you have seen sense enough to acquiesce to my wishes...'

His breath was soft on her skin, his lips warm as they touched the palm, and Suki knew a frightened feeling of being dragged into a sensual trap from which there could be no painless escape.

Hastily, she pulled her hand away and gave him a very frosty look. 'You've made it perfectly clear what it is that you want from me, Pasquale, but I'm warning you that you won't get it.'

'Oh, really?' he mocked.

'You'd better believe it!' And, her head held as proudly as the figurehead of a ship, she swept past him and out of the office, past Carly and the silver-haired lawyer, who still looked in a total state of shock.

Carly leapt forward. 'Suki!' she exclaimed. 'For God's sake...'

But Suki didn't look back as she heard Pasquale's deep voice saying smoothly, 'I apologise for having kept you both waiting. If you'd like to return to the office, we can discuss the contract at length, since Miss Franklin has rescinded her earlier decision and has now happily agreed to honour the agreement.'

*Happily*! If only they knew! Suki kept her face stiff and set until she was outside the Formidable building and had hailed a taxi.

And it wasn't until she had collapsed onto the back seat that she was able to give in to the feelings of impotence and anger which had built to a peak inside her, and she drummed violently at her purple suede clutch-bag as if it were Pasquale's chest she was beating.

It was ten to eight. The stylist had just left and Suki studied herself in her bedroom mirror while she waited for the car which would take her to the Press launch. But even she was unprepared for the impact of the gown she had been given to wear for her debut as the Formidable girl.

Like most models, she was riddled with self-doubts about her appearance, waiting for the day when someone told her that it had all been a big joke, that she wasn't beautiful at all. When she looked in the mirror she usually saw only the flaws in her looks—much, much too tall, with too long legs and the rather narrow hips over-emphasising the surprising lushness of her breasts. But tonight even she found it difficult to fault her appearance.

Her hair spilled down her back in a fiery blur of auburn waves, and the heavy lids of her amber eyes had been cleverly frosted with silver. And the gown itself was exquisite, though where it clung it really *did* cling, emphasising almost in-decently the swell of her breasts and snaking silkily down over her hips. It was the kind of dress that if you had gained even a kilogram of excess weight would define the fact with cruel clarity, she thought, never so glad of the taut flatness of her stomach as she was now.

The sharp ring of the doorbell disturbed her reverie, and she peered through the peephole to see a uniformed chauffeur standing outside.

She opened the door, and the man flashed an identification card. 'Miss Franklin?' he asked.

'That's me!' She gave him a bright smile—after all, it wasn't the poor driver's fault that she was attending this wretched Press launch under such duress!

'The car is waiting downstairs to take you to the hotel,' he told her.

'Thanks. I'll be right down.' Feeling a sudden kinship with the Christians who had been fed to the lions, Suki pulled the matching silver-threaded shawl around her bare shoulders, and followed the chauffeur downstairs and outside into the dark golden summer evening, where a Daimler sat gleaming at the kerbside.

The driver opened the back door and Suki stepped inside the car, but the door had closed behind her before she realised that there was another occupant, and even though the shaded windows meant that the light was comparatively dim she knew immediately just who was re-clining against the soft leather seat, watching her from between lazy, narrowed eyes.

Her heart started thumping as her eyes became accustomed to the light and she saw just what his physique could do for a formal dinner-jacket and snowy-white shirt. It really was unfair—a man as unscrupulous as this man simply didn't deserve to look *that* good. She slid into the corner, as far away from him as possible, and gave him a frosty look.

'Good evening, Suki,' he said softly as the car purred into life and pulled away from the kerb.

'Well, what a surprise!' she said coolly, though her pulse continued to race. 'And a singularly unwelcome one, too. Tell me, Pasquale, do you intend to accompany me on *all* my official engagements?'

'Perhaps,' he answered, unperturbed, a faint smile playing about the corners of his mouth. 'And almost certainly if you are going to look as breathtaking as you do in that dress.'

The murmured compliment, and the slow, appraising look which accompanied it, made her senses fizzle like static electricity. It didn't seem to matter a jot that Pasquale was her enemy, that she disliked him intensely, and that he had nefarious designs on her, because her body, if nothing else, jolted into life when she saw him, welcomed the sight of him with a delight which was causing a feeling of delectable tension to invade her blood.

She tried hard to behave as she would towards any other business acquaintance. Friendly, but *distant*. 'It *is* a beautiful dress,' she conceded. 'You have a very talented stylist.'

He smiled at the polite and stilted tone of her voice. 'Yes. She brought a number of gowns, but the moment I saw that one...'

There was something darkly proprietorial about the way he said it, and Suki's heart thumped painfully. 'You mean that you—*you* chose it?' she queried in disbelief.

'Of course.'

The thought of him selecting the dress which now lay next to her naked skin and very little else made her cheeks flame with an excitement she was bitterly ashamed of, and she was grateful for the dim light of the car. She waited until the heat had left her face before demanding, 'And is that normal practice for you? To choose what your models wear?'

'What do you think?' he answered obliquely.

She was finding it very difficult even to breathe normally right then, let alone *think*. 'I really have no idea,' she answered frostily. 'That's why I'm asking.'

She saw his mouth soften from its cynical hardness, saw his eyes grow impossibly dark, and she knew that at that moment he was aching for her, just as much as she ached for him.

'No, of course I don't normally choose. But the moment I saw this...I wanted to see what you looked like in it. I imagined the contrast of the silver with the gold glitter of those eyes which promise a man so much. I wanted to see the silk caressing the softness of your skin. Because I knew that you would be sensational wearing it; utterly sensational,' he murmured. 'And I was right, wasn't I, Suki? So right...'

Suki had been flattered and complimented by many men in the course of her modelling career, and yet nothing had ever made her heart beat as quickly as it was now, at Pasquale's candidly sexual tribute. And it brought it slamming home that that was all she was to him. Nothing more than a body he wanted to conquer.

She felt her heart clenching as she recognised dully how much it *hurt* that Pasquale should think of her in that way, and that way only. Her breathing was shallow as she attempted to cut him down to size.

'I feel I ought to warn you that making me lose my temper, which I am extremely close to doing, is hardly going to be conducive to getting good photographs of the Formidable woman. So if it is your intention to make me feel like some object you've bought, every time we have the misfortune to meet, then I'd strongly advise against it.'

He shook his head. 'Not at all. It is my intention to have you admit that you want me to kiss you,' he parried softly, and his remark drew her eyes inexorably towards his mouth. 'How about right now, Suki?'

His head was near enough that if he bent forward just a little then their mouths would collide in a soft, sensual encounter. Suki saw the glitter in his dark eyes, and felt her lips part as if some unseen finger had prised them open. Instinctively, she shrank even further away from him, sinking back into the soft leather of the seat, daring him, just *daring* him to try... and she clenched her small fist on top of her silk-covered thigh in preparation.

He smiled as he observed the movement. 'But we wouldn't want to smudge your lipstick, now would we? So we'll postpone that very enjoyable diversion until later. It will be something to look forward to.'

'Like hell!' she spat, like a cat confronted by water.

'More like heaven, I suspect,' he countered on a note of sexy promise.

She searched around desperately for a suitable put-down, but didn't get the chance to use one, because Pasquale changed the tone of the conversation completely, his dark eyebrows meeting in an impatient frown as he clipped out, 'I had a meeting with your brother this afternoon.'

This sounds ominous, thought Suki gloomily. 'Oh?' she said lightly. 'And how was he?'

He continued to frown. 'He was stinking of booze. In the middle of the day,' he added repressively.

'I am not my brother's keeper,' she said. And then, in an effort to distract him, she asked, 'How did you get on with him?'

He shook his head like a disillusioned schoolteacher. 'Frankly, I'm surprised that he's managed to stay in business a *day*, let alone eight years. The man's an absolute liability!'

'There's no need to be quite so offensive!' defended Suki, unable to stop the guilt rushing through her because secretly she tended to agree with Pasquale's every word. 'He tries very hard.'

'He's certainly very trying,' said Pasquale, deadpan.

'And *you're* just showing off your English!' observed Suki acidly as the bright lights of Harrods illuminated the faint smile that her last remark had provoked.

'The most disturbing thing,' continued Pasquale, 'is that he simply doesn't seem to have any grasp of the most fundamental concepts of business. He just looked at me blankly when I mentioned supply and demand and a sympathetic cash flow.'

'That's because *he* didn't have the benefit of doing a business management course at Harvard! Piers inherited the company when my father died, when he was only twenty, just in case you didn't know.'

'Yes, of course I knew,' he said softly. 'And he told me that your mother died last year. I was sorry to hear that, Suki—very sorry indeed.'

She turned to face him. She could bear anything, she thought, but not that soft, almost gentle voice which mimicked the finer human feelings and not just the desire which he felt for her. She swiftly turned her head to stare fixedly out of the window, so that he would not see the sudden moistness in her eyes, and she had time to recover her composure before she heard him tapping on the smoked-glass partition in front of which the driver sat. The electrically controlled panel moved aside immediately.

'Just draw up here, would you?' asked Pasquale. 'I intend taking Miss Franklin round by a side-entrance.' He looked down at her. 'Are you OK now?'

She nodded, surprised at the concern underlying his question. 'Don't you want to make the big entrance, then?' she asked curiously, and he shook his head.

'There's usually a scrum of photographers. Sometimes it can get out of hand, as I'm sure you know, and there's absolutely no need for you to have to fight your way through them all.'

She felt ridiculously touched by his solicitude, even though he spoilt it rather by murmuring, 'Besides, the element of surprise is always an advantage, don't you think, Suki?' However, she didn't get a chance to object, for suddenly she found herself being handed out of the car and he caught her hand in his and led her through a discreet side-door. For a few moments their palms were in contact, his fingers firmly gripping hers, and it took everything she had to stop her own fingers from curling possessively around his hand.

And it wasn't until they were speeding upwards in one of the service lifts he'd managed to locate that she noticed that he was smiling.

It was quite something, that smile.

'You're *enjoying* this!' she accused. 'Aren't you?'

There was a pause. His face was quite serious for a moment. 'More than I would have imagined, little one. I thought, perhaps foolishly, that your capitulation would be instant,' he murmured. 'The signs in France were so promising.'

Suki was scarcely able to believe her ears. 'The signs in France were so promising'. Oh, *were* they? So he thought that her 'capitulation would be instant', *did* he? 'Of all the most arrogant, conceited things I've ever heard—'

'I had no idea, *cara*,' he interrupted shamelessly, his eyes never leaving the curve of her lips, 'that you were going to fight me all the way, or indeed how much I would enjoy the fight, the anticipation of victory.'

She *could* protest. She *could* start twittering on about honour and decency and the shameful expectations of brutish men like him.

She *could*.

And he, no doubt—arrogant beast that he was—would indulgently smile and nod as he listened to all her protestations.

Before kissing her to death.

Suki shuddered. What did they say about actions speaking louder than words? If he attempted to take her into his arms again she would be as responsive as a block of ice. She clamped her lips together in a tight line, which was exactly what she was intending to do if he tried to kiss her.

The dark eyes mocked her as the lift doors slid open. Along the corridor Suki could see a scrum of photographers waiting.

Pasquale put a hand at the small of her back and looked down at her. 'Ready?' he asked.

'For *anything*,' she replied, and as their eyes clashed with the light of battle her heart began to pound painfully because she heard the sultry throb of a woman's voice calling his name.

# CHAPTER SIX

'PASQUALE, *darling*! So there you are!' And an imperious-looking woman in her late twenties, with sleek blue-black hair, came bearing down on them. She was wearing a military-style scarlet dress which positively *exuded* class, and she made Suki, in the slinky silver silk, feel half-naked in comparison.

She rarely met women other than models who equalled her in height, but this woman certainly did. She also seemed to know Pasquale very well indeed, since she was proffering him alternate cool, pale cheeks, and Suki watched, fascinated, while he gave her three kisses.

'Where the hell did you spring from?' the woman asked, adding something in Italian in a low, sexy undertone, but Pasquale shook his head.

'We took the service lift. And Suki doesn't speak any Italian, so we'd better not,' he said smoothly.

The woman held two beautifully manicured hands in the air. 'Of course she doesn't—how silly of me!'

Suki glared but said nothing.

Pasquale smiled. 'Have you two actually met before?'

'No-o,' said the woman, and gave Suki a cold scrutiny from head to toe. 'I don't *think* so.'

'Suki,' said Pasquale, 'this is Stacey Lomas. She heads Lomas & Lomas, the advertising agency I happen to use—'

'For more years than I care to remember!' trilled Stacey, batting her eyelids like crazy.

OK, so you know him pretty well—I get the message, thought Suki, masking her strange feeling of disappointment behind a bright smile.

'And Stacey,' continued Pasquale, 'may I present the new Formidable girl? Of course, you'll recognise Suki from her portfolio.'

'Of course,' echoed Stacey, her elegant eyebrows ever so slightly raised in a gesture of surprise, as though Suki in the flesh bore little resemblance to the Suki of her portfolio photographs.

'Hello,' smiled Suki, thinking that you wouldn't need to hold a doctorate in human behaviour to realise that the elegant Ms Lomas was very keen on Signor Caliandro. Very keen indeed. That much was obvious from the amused glances she kept throwing him, and the secret little smile which played around her rather sultry, scarlet-painted lips.

'Hello, Suki,' responded Stacey at last, very coolly. 'Well, now you're here, we can get started. I guess we'd better introduce you to the gentlemen from the press corps.'

'Gentlemen?' joked Suki. 'From the *press corps*? Now this I have to see!'

She saw Pasquale smile, but she moved away, eager to begin, glad to be able to do what she had been employed for: sell the product. It meant that she could slip into automatic pilot, doing her job with the utmost professionalism which had always been her trademark, instead of thinking and wondering just how far the relationship between Pasquale and Stacey Lomas went. And if he was unscrupulous enough to want more than one mistress at the same time...

A large function room had been set aside at the Granchester Hotel and had been completely decorated in gold and blue, which were the colours which adorned the Formidable packaging.

And they'd certainly gone to town, thought Suki admiringly as she looked around, if perhaps a little over the top...

There were gold and blue ribbons and streamers, and gold and blue metallic balloons with the legend 'C'est Formidable' printed on every one. There was every kind of blue flower imaginable—delphiniums, cornflowers, irises, hyacinths—all standing clustered in flamboyant golden bowls which were dotted strategically around the room.

And on a table next to the stand which displayed bottles of Formidable perfume, as well as all their make-up and toiletry ranges, were blue-stemmed glasses filled with champagne, which the press corps were quaffing back like men who had been denied hard liquor for years.

'Would you like some champagne?' asked Pasquale.

She shook her head. 'Not when I'm working— thanks.'

'Then could I ask you to come and stand over here?' interjected Stacey hurriedly. 'And we'll put you to work.'

Like a beast of burden, thought Suki crossly, though her bright smile never faltered as she moved fluidly across the room behind the advertising boss. She resented Stacey Lomas's implication that she was nothing more than an airhead, which was unusual. All the normal preconceptions which people had about professional models didn't normally bother her. After all, she wasn't trying to impress anyone. She earned a generous amount of money and she paid her taxes. People liked her or they didn't, and she could take or leave their opinion.

So what was it about Stacey Lomas?

Her apparently close relationship with Pasquale?

The hell it was! Suki tossed her auburn hair in abandon and fifty flash bulbs exploded into incandescent blue-white light.

She was aware that Pasquale was there in the room with her and it affected her performance intensely. She played it like she'd never played it before. He'd wanted her to sell the product, so sell it she damned well would!

He'd wanted glamour and he'd wanted sex appeal—well, look out, Pasquale, she thought wickedly—here it comes!

She pouted. She smiled seductively. She playfully hid behind her long curtain of auburn hair. She slitted her amber eyes so that they gleamed with promise. And the press corps went mad, whistling their appreciation and snapping away like mad.

When she had given them every photo they could possibly want—plus a few more besides—the session was called to a halt. Suki stepped off the small platform, close to where Pasquale stood, and she was taken aback by the thunderous look of anger on his face as his dark eyes clashed with hers.

*Now* what was the matter with him, the moody brute?

And who cares? she thought defiantly as she slung the silver wrap over her shoulders.

Stacey was smiling like a woman who had just won the lottery. 'Pasquale, *cara*,' she was saying. 'I'm starving. Have you eaten yet?'

'No,' he answered tersely, his face tense as he continued to cast daggers in Suki's direction.

'Then let's try that new Thai restaurant in Soho, shall we? I've heard it's excellent.'

'So have I, but I'm afraid it will have to be another time,' he answered smoothly, but there was still an abrasive glitter in his eyes.

'Oh?' Stacey pouted, the pout looking more petulant than seductive, thought Suki with sudden, triumphant glee.

'Sorry.' He shrugged broad, elegantly clad shoulders. 'I'm catching a flight to New York first thing, and I need to catch up on sleep.'

Suki couldn't help wondering just *why* he needed to catch up on sleep, but blocked the thought in an instant. His nocturnal habits were nothing to do with her. 'Is the car still outside?' she asked him neutrally. 'Because I'd like to go home now.'

'I'll see you downstairs,' he said.

Suki shook her head. 'There's really no need,' she replied, just *daring* him to challenge her.

He did.

'Oh, but I insist,' he said softly, and there was an edge of unmistakable menace in his voice.

Short of having a ding-dong with him which would no doubt enthral the remaining photographers who were finishing off the last of the champagne, there seemed little alternative but to go with him. And Suki did derive some small amount of satisfaction from the look of fury which Stacey Lomas sent flashing in her direction.

This time they used the main lift, and as there were two other people in it they said nothing, but Suki could sense the anger in Pasquale; his normally relaxed body was held rigid and his face was tight with tension.

In the lobby she turned to him. 'If you'll just point me in the direction of the car—'

But he did no such thing. He firmly took hold of her hand and led her towards the revolving glass doors.

'What—the hell do you think you're doing?' she spluttered.

'Taking you home.'

'I don't want to go home with you!'

'Tough!' came his uncompromising reply. Gosh, but he could sound like an American gangster sometimes!

Even worse was to come.

The gleaming Daimler she had arrived in was nowhere to be seen. One of the hotel's doormen was just getting out of a long, gun-metal-grey sports car, and was handing a set of keys to Pasquale.

'Your car, sir,' he said, then grinned. 'She handles like a dream!'

For a moment, Pasquale was charm personified. 'Doesn't she? Thanks very much.' He smiled lazily, and discreetly handed the doorman a whopping great tip.

Pasquale opened the passenger door. 'Get in,' he said shortly.

Suki opened her mouth to refuse, then hastily shut it when she saw the grim line of determination on his face which was masquerading as a mouth. Besides which, she was quite enjoying seeing him in such a temper. She didn't know what had caused it, but it seemed strangely out of character for the formidably controlled and controlling Pasquale!

The car roared off sounding like a schoolboy's dream, and Suki stole a glance at that stark, uncompromising profile.

'Would you mind explaining—?'

'Shut up,' he told her.

'But—'

'Not *now*, Suki! I'm trying to keep my eyes on the damned road!'

'Do you realise you're crunching the gears?' she asked sweetly, and saw his knuckles whiten in response.

'Don't say another word,' he grated in a scarcely audible voice.

'Or what?'

'Or I may just lose my temper,' he warned her.

'And is that supposed to frighten me?' she taunted.

'Yes,' he gritted as he skidded up outside her block with a screech. 'If you happen to be a sensible girl.'

Suki unclipped her seat belt. 'Well, thanks very much for the pleasant chat,' she mocked. '*Now* what do you think you're doing?'

He swung himself out of the car and came round to open her door. 'I should think it's very obvious what I'm doing,' he said. 'I'm coming inside with you.'

His face was dark and determined. Her heart thumped. 'Oh, no, you're not!'

'Just try stopping me,' he said silkily.

The most bizarre thing was that she wasn't frightened. Far from it. And she was honest enough to admit to herself what the source of her thundering heart was.

Excitement.

She gazed into the glittering blackness of his eyes. 'You think I wouldn't dare?' she challenged.

'I have no idea. I should be delighted to see you try,' he answered, with a quiet determination which renewed the racing of her heart.

And he didn't even wait until her front door was closed before pulling her ruthlessly into his arms, kicking the door shut behind them with a deafening slam.

'Been watching too many cowboy movies?' she taunted breathlessly, refusing to be intimidated by his cavalier behaviour, or lulled by that strong hand which clasped her waist so firmly.

His eyes were blazing down at her. 'How the hell could you do it?' he demanded harshly.

Now she really *was* confused. 'Do what?'

'Behave like that!'

'Like what?'

'Don't play the innocent with me!' he exploded dramatically and his accent deepened. 'You know damned well what I'm talking about!'

*'What?'*

'My God,' he breathed. 'The way you were tonight; the way you looked. Those lips, those eyes, that body in that dress—'

'Which *you* chose!' she retorted in disbelief.

'Yes, I chose, and, Mother of God, what a fool I was,' he said, half to himself, before renewing his onslaught. 'You looked like you were making love to every man in the room! Was that your intention?'

'Oh, for goodness' *sake*!' Suki tore herself out of his arms. 'Just what did you expect? You employed me to help sell your product, didn't you? You wanted me to be glamorous and to use sex

appeal—those were *your* words, if you remember! *Yes*, I flirted! And *yes*, I looked provocative—because that is specifically what you
asked for, Pasquale. And models do that kind of
work all the time, and don't pretend you're so
naïve and so stupid as not to know that! It's
totally harmless—'

'Is it?' he asked dangerously.

'Of course it is!'

'And if I hadn't been there, don't you think
that some of those photographers—some of them
the worse for drink—would have been hanging
around, waiting to take you home? Would you
have gone with any of them, Suki?'

She was so angry that she lifted her hand and
slapped his face hard, but he didn't flinch; he
didn't react at all, save for a brief flash of fire
in his dark eyes and the harsh tightening of his
mouth.

'How *dare* you?' she said, in a voice so shaky
that her words sounded almost indistinct. 'Apart
from the fact that I'm perfectly capable of saying
no, most of those guys are happily married with
children—and those who aren't know that it's just
a job. I doubt whether anyone there would have
resorted to the kind of primitive behaviour which
*you* seem to indulge in—namely dragging me off
in your car like something out of the Stone Age!'

'And do you think that I normally behave like
this?' he demanded, in a strained kind of voice.

Suki angrily pushed a strand of hair off her
forehead. 'How should I know how you *normally* behave, when what's normal for you seems

pretty eccentric to me? Normal for you seems to be getting a foothold into my brother's business and using that to bribe me into working for you. That is, of course, when you aren't threatening me with breach of contract...'

He shook his dark head. 'No. Forget that.'

She narrowed her eyes suspiciously. 'Forget what?'

He sighed. 'I won't sue you for breach of contract. I made you take the job under duress. You don't want to work for me, and you will no longer have to. I'm dropping you as the Formidable girl.'

Suki blinked in astonishment. 'But financially that could be disastrous for you—you've just introduced me to the *Press*, for heaven's sake!'

He shrugged his broad shoulders philosophically. 'My bank balance can withstand the occasional mistake.'

Suki frowned. This was a complete turn-around. 'And what about Piers, and Franklin Motors?'

'Don't worry—I won't go back on my word to invest in your brother's business. I shall follow that through.'

His words sank in, and she realised that here she had the opportunity to be free of him. And her reaction to that was not at all what she would have predicted.

'You are not,' she said coolly, 'doing any such thing.'

'What?' he said softly, his eyes flaring, as if he couldn't believe what she had just said.

'You are not dropping me as the Formidable girl, because I've decided that I happen to quite like it. And if you do, then I shall sue *you* for breach of contract. Do you understand *that*, Pasquale?'

There was a stunned silence and then he did something totally unexpected.

He laughed.

And Suki almost melted under the impact of that laugh.

'Ah, Suki,' he murmured appreciatively. 'I see that I have found myself a truly worthy adversary.' He paused, and gave her a discerning look. 'Is it intentional, I wonder?' he quizzed softly. 'Do you know what you're doing?'

'About what?' she asked, momentarily perplexed. 'You're speaking in riddles.'

He smiled. 'Do you realise that the more you fight and resist me, the more I want you—?'

'Yes, I know,' she cut in acidly. 'The more you want me to be your mistress! A loathsome word!'

To her surprise, he nodded, and his face became serious. 'I agree, *bella*. And I was wrong. Very wrong.'

'Wrong?' Suki found it very difficult to take in the fact that Pasquale was admitting fault!

'Mmm,' he murmured. 'A mistress is someone who can be bought, owned—an inappropriate word for someone as fiery as you, Suki. For, even if he held you in chains, I can imagine no man ever owning you. No, I can think of a far better description for you than mistress.'

Somehow she managed to keep her face neutral, even though her heart was racing like crazy. 'Oh, really? I can't wait to hear it.'

*'Lover,'* he whispered, in a voice of dark velvet. 'Will you? Be my lover, Suki?' He caressed the word with his mouth as he reached out and pulled her back into his arms, his fingers beginning to delicately caress the narrow span of her waist.

Disappointment stole over her as she banished for ever the romantic fantasy of what she had foolishly been imagining that he was about to say. Not something which sounded as expendable as 'lover', anyway. She lifted her chin proudly. 'No, I won't!' she said quietly, and with the most monumental effort she pulled away from him and went to stand next to the window.

'I don't believe you,' he said simply. 'Why are you denying what we both feel? Fighting it so hard, when I know and you know that you want more than anything else to give in to it?'

Suki turned abruptly away, hating what his words did to her equilibrium, unwilling to face him for fear that he would read the vulnerability in her eyes. He was right. She *did* want him— wanted him in a way she had never wanted a man before. But what he was offering wasn't enough— could never be enough: the temporary lover, to be replaced when he had tired of her.

'No, Pasquale,' she answered in a low voice.

'And yet you will continue to be the Formidable girl, knowing that our paths will constantly cross. Have you asked yourself why?

Don't you imagine that our continued proximity will wear down your already weak defences?'

She gave him a cool look. 'Is that a challenge?'

'I'm not entirely sure,' he murmured. 'Will you accept it, if it is?'

She shook her head. 'I'm too tired for all this game-playing.' And then she saw the faint red mark on one olive cheek and her own face paled. 'Your cheek is marked,' she said, biting her bottom lip in horror. 'I'm sorry, Pasquale—I should never have hit you.'

He shrugged. 'I deserved it—my criticisms were unjust. You were only doing your job.' His dark eyes blazed. 'I was jealous, you see.'

And that means *nothing*, Suki assured herself.

'But you can make it up to me if you like,' he said softly.

'I can imagine how,' she responded acidly.

He raised his dark brows speculatively. 'By making me some coffee,' he said. 'I could kill for a cup.'

And to her consternation he allowed his long-limbed frame to settle itself languidly on one of her sofas and smiled beguilingly up at her.

She stared at him, taking in that easy assurance he wore like a second skin, and she couldn't help laughing, despite her misgivings. 'All that—and you ask me for coffee! You're impossible—do you know that?'

'It has been said,' he conceded, and the look he gave her was loaded with amusement, and *that*, Suki discovered, was a far more powerful weapon in his armoury than his potent sexual charisma. Because shared humour could somehow be incredibly intimate, too...

'How do you take your coffee?' she heard herself saying.

'As it comes,' he smiled. 'Thank you.'

'And if you're about to launch into the charm offensive,' she told him archly, 'then please don't bother.' But she swung out of the room to the sound of his low, mocking laughter.

Suki clattered around in her kitchen, getting down a couple of the bright pottery cups she collected, and which she had brought back from her various travels, wondering what kind of woman would be making coffee for the man she loved to hate. A madwoman, that was who, she told herself with some of her customary humour as she began to grind the coffee-beans. And if she was trying to play games, then she was playing way out of her league with Pasquale.

Still, she tried to reason with herself, perhaps if they did something as civilised as drinking coffee together, then he wouldn't go into caveman mode every time she was around. Perhaps he would stop asking her to become his...

*Lover.*

The word thrilled her yet chilled her. And if it had been anyone else but Pasquale she *might* have felt tempted. But if you took on Pasquale you could guarantee yourself a broken heart, and a broken heart she could do without.

Which left her with the still unanswered question of just *why* she hadn't accepted his offer to terminate her Formidable contract. Was it

stubborn pride—wanting to prove to herself, and
to him, that she could resist him? Or was it simply
because she wanted to thwart his wishes?

She shook her head in confusion as she added
a plateful of home-made biscuits to the tray, and
carried it through into the living room, where
Pasquale had moved from the sofa and was
standing studying one of her paintings as intently
as if he were about to undergo an examination
on it.

Remember, she reminded herself as he turned
towards her. Be civilised. Drink some coffee with
him, European style. Do that and it may arouse
the chivalry in him, rather than the passion.

It seemed that it did. He took the tray from
her protesting hands and put it down on a small
table which was next to one of the two ice-blue
sofas which stood facing each other.

She warily watched him sit on one sofa and
she chose the one opposite.

She was not used to men indolently lounging
in her flat, and yet Pasquale looked so *right*
sitting there, she thought as she poured their
coffee. So dark and so powerful, and yet at the
same time so graciously at ease. He took the cup
from her. 'Thanks,' he said, and observed her
from beneath dark, thick lashes as he sipped the
fragrant brew. 'Excellent coffee,' he said, on a
note of unconscious wonder.

'You mean for an English woman?'

'I'm sorry—that was extremely pompous of
me,' he said.

'Your English is excellent,' she remarked mischievously.

His eyes gleamed. *'Touché!'*

She realised with an unwelcome shock that she found him as stimulating intellectually as physically. Which didn't help. I don't want to find him any *more* attractive than I already do, she thought plaintively. 'Would you like a biscuit?' she enquired hurriedly, proffering the plate.

'Thank you.' He took one, bit into it and raised one dark eyebrow. 'Also very good,' he observed. 'You didn't bake them yourself by any chance?'

'Didn't I? What suppositions you make, Pasquale,' she reprimanded mockingly. 'Actually I did, and there's no need to sound surprised.'

'Oh, but I am.'

'Why?'

A broad olive hand indicated the room with a broad sweep. 'Your whole flat is a surprise.' His gesture took in the deep red walls which provided such a dramatic backdrop for her paintings, the clutter of bright, beautiful vases which adorned the mantelpiece, the brightly embroidered cushions she'd brought back from India which should have clashed violently with the cerise sofa but somehow set it off magnificently.

'In what way?'

He shrugged his broad shoulders. 'This room,' he said, 'is exactly the opposite of what I would have expected of you.'

'And just what did you expect?'

'Something minimalist, elegant, streamlined. Certainly not this.'

'This being . . . ?'

He shrugged again. 'It is wild and it is beautiful, but it is not safe. It is a room into which the guiding hand of an interior designer would never be admitted. And it is not the room of an independent career-woman,' he stated finally.

She suspected that he had more experience than most of analysing the decor of women's homes. 'And that's how you see me, is it, Pasquale—as an independent career-woman?'

'Of course. Isn't that what you are?'

She supposed that she was. But it didn't sound like her at all—it somehow had a very cold-sounding ring to it. She made a restless little movement. 'Sure it is.'

'And yet—' his dark eyes were appreciative '—you grind coffee-beans and you bake biscuits.'

She certainly couldn't let *that* go unremarked upon! 'Well, I *am* a woman,' she purred demurely.

He smiled as he acknowledged the jibe. 'Mmm. You most certainly are,' he murmured. He finished the last of his coffee and leaned back, his dark head resting against the palms of his hands as he studied the walls. 'And you still paint— quite beautifully, in fact.'

She liked his praise of her work, she realised. She liked it very much. 'But why should that surprise you?' she asked. 'I always did paint. Remember?'

The light died in his eyes. 'Yes. I remember. I
thought that you should take it up as a career;
do you remember *that*? But you chose to capi-
talise on your looks instead.'

She bristled indignantly at the implied
criticism. 'That's because modelling pays and
painting doesn't!' she retorted. 'And, unlike you,
I had to go out and earn a living!'

'Is that how you see *me*?' he questioned coolly.
'The poor little rich boy? Perhaps you think that
I was handed everything on a plate? If you do,
Suki, then you are quite wrong.

'My father put me into the business at the
bottom end of the ladder; he wanted to make sure
that I knew every part of how it should be run.
And being the boss's son isn't all roses, you
know. A lot of people resent you for what you
will one day inherit. Inevitably, your position
isolates you. I worked damned hard to build the
business to the level it's at today. I still do,' he
finished, on an odd note.

'You sound bitter,' she said quietly.

'A little. It galls me that so much money has
been eaten up by the greed of my stepmother over
the years, but that, fortunately, will soon be
remedied.'

'Oh?'

He gave her a cruel kind of smile. 'My father
is in the throes of divorcing her. It has taken him
some time, but he has seen the light at last.' The
smile vanished without a trace.

'So in effect you're condemning her just because she got a bit carried away with the credit cards, are you?'

He met her gaze with a steady look. 'Greed is forgivable,' he told her harshly, 'but infidelity is not.'

She was imprisoned in that bright, hard stare. Pasquale would never need fear infidelity, she thought. No woman of his would ever look at another man. 'And your sister?' she asked suddenly. 'How is she these days?'

'Francesca is well—like you, the independent career-woman. She practises law in Rome.'

*Francesca?* Crazy, impetuous Francesca—a *lawyer*? 'Good grief,' said Suki faintly.

'Now *you* sound surprised,' he observed.

'I am. She must have changed a lot.'

'Yes, she has. Changing schools so that she was closer to home was the best thing that could have happened to her.'

She waited for him to rake up her old, supposed sins, but his next words took her completely by surprise.

'Don't you ever long for a real home, Suki?' he probed suddenly. 'With the clutter of a husband and children?'

Something wrenched at her heart as she pictured what he was describing, but the image which stubbornly refused to budge had a male lead who bore an uncanny resemblance to Pasquale, with several dark-eyed children playing around his feet. 'Not really,' she replied, her voice threatening to tremble. 'As you said yourself, I'm an independent career-woman—husband and children don't fit in very well with my kind of work.'

'And is that why you've never married?' he persisted.

No, it wasn't. The reason she'd never married was sitting right opposite her. She'd never married because she'd never met another man to equal him. And the frightening and very real prospect which lay ahead of her was that she probably never would.

'I'm still too busy playing the field,' she lied, and was stunned by the look of anger which began to smoulder in the depths of his eyes.

'Yes, I'll bet you are!' he affirmed harshly.

Civility had just vanished, she realised, and conflict—dear, familiar conflict—had returned with a vengeance to replace it. She hurriedly stood. 'I really must ask you to leave now, Pasquale,' she said with deliberate politeness. 'I'm very tired.'

This time he made no demur. He rose to his feet. 'Thank you for the coffee,' he said with equal courtesy, and moved forward to replace his cup on the tray at exactly the same time as Suki bent to deposit her own, and their fingers unwittingly brushed together.

Suki took a step back, but her legs were suddenly shaky and she might have slipped had not one strong hand whipped out in a lightning-sharp reflex and caught her by the wrist.

Just that brief contact was enough to remind Suki of how devastating his touch could be and her skin seemed to throb with heated blood where he'd touched her.

Could he feel the acceleration of her pulse beneath his fingertips? Was that why he was looking down at her with that odd expression in his eyes, that disturbing softening of the normally hard line of his mouth?

'Thank you,' she said breathlessly, but she made no move to pull away, and he made no move to let her go.

'My pleasure,' he said softly.

Pleasure. It was a word he was comfortable with, familiar with. Pasquale could give her pleasure... untold pleasure. It was hers for the taking; she only had to ask. Involuntarily, the tip of her tongue edged out to slick around her arid lips, and his eyes darkened with desire.

'You must not do such things, *bella mia*,' he reprimanded her softly, his eyes never leaving her mouth, now glossy and trembling from the dark hunger she read on his face. 'Make such gestures... such provocative gestures.' His finger reached up to lightly touch the moist fullness of her bottom lip. 'Unless you are prepared to face the consequences.'

She stared up into his face, dazed and dazzled and entranced by him. He was still, she realised dully, holding her wrist. Oh, for heaven's sake, Suki, she thought despairingly.

She tried to pull away but failed, knowing that it was not his strength to blame, but her own inertia. And suddenly it was too late to move, because his hand had dropped from her mouth and moved to the slender band of her waist, and the rhythmical expertise of his fingers sensuously rubbing against the hopelessly inadequate silver silk was simply too much for her; it felt as though he was touching her bare flesh. God help her, she thought fleetingly as she began to sink helplessly into the sensation.

'Pasquale,' she whispered weakly, all the fight and the lies and the good intentions gone out of her.

'What?' The desire in his voice made it sound like honey trickling slowly over rough gravel.

'Let me—go.'

'In a minute I shall have to, though I am most reluctant to do so. Such a pity that I have to fly to New York tomorrow, *cara*,' he said regretfully. 'However...' and his voice dropped to an irresistible murmur '....I shall leave you something to remember me by. A taste of things to come.' And his eyes glittered as he lowered his mouth to possess hers.

She tried doing what she'd vowed to do much earlier that evening—an age ago—becoming a block of ice in his arms—but the thaw happened within seconds of his soft, sweet touch.

The other thing she had vowed to do was to keep her lips tightly clamped together, but that too proved fruitless, because when he pulled her decisively against the hard, aroused length of his body her lips fluttered open on a sigh, and his tongue penetrated her mouth with an erotic promise of unimaginable delights to come.

She swayed, but he held her firm, and she decided that since she really *was* powerless to resist his kiss, then she might as well do what she really wanted to do.

She kissed him back.

She let her hands slide luxuriously over his broad back, fingering the thick silk of his black dinner-jacket, plucking at it restlessly as if anxious to feel the muscles beneath, and she delighted in the small moan he gave as he deepened the kiss.

She didn't know how long he kissed her for, only that at one point she feared that she might actually faint. 'Pasquale,' she whispered helplessly.

He raised his mouth from hers and looked down into her face. His breathing was almost as unsteady as her own as he took in the hectic flush which stained her high cheekbones, the febrile glitter of her eyes, and the parted, swollen lips which were dark with the pressure of his kiss.

The half-smile he gave then was neither soft nor gentle nor humourless. It was nakedly, unashamedly predatory.

'Yes,' he affirmed, almost harshly, 'I should take you now and quench this heat in my loins which threatens to overwhelm me.' He ceased holding her, and it took all she had not to crumple in a heap at his feet.

And perhaps he guessed that, for he moved a hand again as if to steady her, but mutely she pushed it feebly away, righting herself against the arm of the sofa.

'But I have an early flight,' he continued remorsely. 'And I can promise you one thing...that when I finally gain access to your bed I don't intend to creep out at dawn. I intend to stay there making love to you for just as long as it takes, *cara mia*.'

And the mocking words rang in her ears as he left and quietly closed the door behind him.

# CHAPTER SEVEN

IN THEORY, with Pasquale in New York, Suki's life should have been less stressful.

But that was in theory, and the reality was startlingly, frighteningly different.

She found that she missed him. In fact, if she was being painfully and brutally honest with herself—she missed him quite badly.

She did two shoots for Formidable but found herself constantly glancing around the studio, as if hoping to catch a glimpse of that dark, proud head.

She lost her appetite, her sense of humour and she couldn't paint. Staring aimlessly out of the window one sunny morning, four days after he had gone, she decided to ring her sister-in-law to ask if she could take her young nephew out for the day. It would give Kirstie a break, and Toby was such fun to be with, he'd be bound to take her mind off Pasquale.

There was no reply at home, so Suki decided to ring Piers at the office to ask if he knew where they were.

She dialled his direct line, and almost dropped the receiver when she heard a familiar deep voice say, 'Yes?'

He's back from New York, she thought, with a dull ache where her heart should have been.

He's back, and he hasn't been in touch, was her *stupid* reaction to hearing him speak.

'Hello?' he said, a touch impatiently.

'Hello,' echoed Suki eventually, when she had convinced herself that it would be childish to simply replace the receiver.

'Suki?' he said instantly. 'Is that you?'

'Yes, it's me. Is Piers there, please?'

'He is.'

There was a pause. 'May I speak to him?'

'In a moment. How are you?'

He sounded as though he was genuinely interested. He sounded as though he'd missed *her*, too. Oh, Suki, she thought, he probably had plenty of female diversions in New York. 'I'm fine,' she said, rather stiltedly. 'How are you?'

He laughed, as if he found her formal tone amusing. 'Tired. Very tired. It was a busy trip.' His voice deepened. 'Did you miss me?' he asked softly, putting words to her errant thoughts with shocking perception.

'Sure, Pasquale. Like the proverbial hole in the head!'

But he simply gave a low, mocking laugh. 'I hear from Lomas that your two shoots for Formidable went very well.'

'So they tell me.'

'Will you have dinner with me tonight?' he asked suddenly.

I—I'd love to, she was about to say as common sense momentarily flew swiftly out of the window, but she brought herself up sharply and pushed the temptation away as firmly as if it had been a cream cake and she'd needed to lose a kilo. Besides, it was easy to refuse him when she didn't have to look into those devilish black eyes of his. 'I can't,' she said coolly.

She heard the frown in his voice. 'A date?' he queried abruptly.

'I'm busy,' she said evasively.

'Too busy to cancel, I suppose?' he drawled, the familiar arrogance back again.

'Has a woman ever said no to you before?' she queried in disbelief.

'You wouldn't really want me to answer that, would you, Suki?'

'Why should it bother *me* what you answer?' she returned frostily. 'Your private life is of no interest to me whatsoever.'

He laughed softly. 'No?'

'No. And in answer to your question—I wouldn't dream of cancelling,' she said witheringly. 'That would be so rude, don't you think?'

'You're absolutely right, of course,' he agreed. 'I didn't expect you to—and I'd have been disappointed if you'd done so. It doesn't matter. I can wait.'

'But you told me you weren't a patient man,' she reminded him, wondering how he managed to make what was essentially a threat sound like the most enticing promise. 'Have you forgotten?'

'No, I haven't forgotten, but maybe I was wrong. I seem to be discovering all kind of things about myself, Suki. Like how stimulating I find it to do battle with you.'

'Oh, do you?' she said repressively. 'Well, I'd like to speak to my brother now, if you don't mind!'

Again she heard the smile in his voice; she could even imagine it creasing his arrogant, kissable mouth. 'Sure. I'll put him on. I'll see you at the launch tomorrow.' He hesitated. 'Enjoy your date,' he said softly, and then he was gone.

'Suki?'

It was Piers's voice. 'Hello, Piers,' she said. 'How are things?'

His voice sounded strained. 'Fine!' he answered, in a tone which belied his words. Then his voice lowered. 'I'm bloody exhausted, to be honest. Don't worry—he's gone out of the room. This Caliandro chap thinks that starting work before eight in the morning is quite normal.'

'But it is, for a lot of people,' Suki pointed out.

'But I'm an *executive*, honey-child! I'm the flaming managing director, for heaven's sake!'

'But the title will mean nothing if you don't have a viable company!' said Suki impatiently.

'I know! I know,' he sighed. 'Don't nag me, Sukes. It just takes a bit of getting used to, that's all. Now, what can I do for you?'

'I was wondering if you knew where Kirstie is? I tried calling her at home but there was no reply.'

'She's taken Toby down to the health centre first thing—'

'He's not ill, is he?'

'No, he's fine. Just a routine assessment. She should be back by ten. What did you want to speak to her about?' he asked suspiciously.

'Well, certainly not about you! I was hoping to take Toby to the zoo.'

'Gosh, he'd love that, Suki,' said Piers appreciatively. 'And so would Kirstie.'

'And so would I!' laughed Suki. 'I love zoos, but I rarely get a chance to indulge myself—you really need a child in tow!'

'Well, if you take him there on a real, live London double-decker bus he'll be your friend for life! We keep promising him a ride on one, but we've never quite got round to it.' And then he said something which Suki couldn't quite catch.

'What was that?' she said.

'Oh, nothing. Pasquale just walked back into the office and was intrigued by my conversation.'

'Oh,' said Suki flatly, and felt the briefest pang of jealousy. Just because her brother had easy access to the man she claimed to hate?

Please!

'Mmm,' carried on Piers, as though she hadn't spoken. 'It seems that *he's* never been on a double-decker bus either.'

'Really?' said Suki in a sarcastic voice that she hoped was loud enough for the man in question to hear!

She waited until ten then rang her sister-in-law, who was delighted to take her up on her offer, so Suki slung on a pair of old jeans and a white ruffled shirt, and set off to collect Toby from the pretty tree-lined road in Primrose Hill where they lived.

'Arnie Sooty!' shrieked Toby with excitement as she walked into the playroom, and hurled himself into her arms with all the speed and enthusiasm of a young dynamo. Suki picked her nephew up and cuddled him.

'Want to come to the zoo with me?' she asked.

'Big lions?'

'Lions and tigers and elephants and polar bears, too!'

'And snakes?' he said hopefully.

Suki shuddered. 'Unfortunately, yes, Toby—there will be snakes.'

Suki watched while Toby wriggled out of her arms and banged on a drum excitedly.

'He gets more like Piers every day!' she told Kirstie.

'Piers says he's got your mother's nose, though,' said Kirstie softly.

'Mmm.' For a moment Suki was pensive, a fleeting sadness showing briefly on her lovely face. 'It's strange, isn't it, how familial likeness gallops through the generations? Though perhaps it's not so strange,' she added thoughtfully. 'That's our little bit of immortality, isn't it?'

Kirstie sent her a curious look. 'You sounded quite wistful there, Suki. You're not getting broody, are you?'

Suki forced a laugh as again that disturbing image of Pasquale as father to her child leapt to the forefront of her mind. 'No, I'm not! Toby is my bit of motherhood by proxy, and that suits me down to the ground!'

'There are four nappies, his book and his baby beaker in here,' said Kirstie as she handed over the bag she'd packed. 'Do you want to take the pushchair?'

'I'd better, hadn't I?'

But a hundred yards down the road her nephew firmly decided that he wanted to walk, so Suki folded up the pushchair and carried it underneath one arm, while Toby clung onto her hand and toddled alongside her. And then Suki's steps faltered as her eyes focused on the tall figure at the end of the street who was standing watching them.

He began walking towards her, his dark eyes never leaving her face, and her heart gave an unsteady lurch as each step brought him closer to her.

He was wearing a white T-shirt which was tucked into black jeans which moulded the narrow line of his hips, and the casual clothes made him look unfamiliarly carefree and young. The T-shirt was clinging indecently to his chest, outrageously defining the solid sinew and muscle which lay beneath, and Suki felt the first, inevitable shimmerings of desire beginning to stir.

She swallowed, momentarily rendered motionless by the sheer force of his physical impact, feasting her eyes on him as though it were the first time she had ever seen him. Four days, she realised, could be one hell of a long time.

'Hello,' he said softly.

Her heart seemed to slow before picking up speed again, and she felt her cheeks flame as they stared at each other.

'Do you know,' he said, 'I don't think I've ever met a woman who blushes quite as easily as you do?'

'Deceptive things, appearances, aren't they?' she mocked.

'Are they?' His eyes gleamed. 'So *did* you miss me?'

'What do *you* think?' she returned sweetly.

'I suspect that you have. Very much. I think that you've probably lain awake at nights unable to get me out of your mind. Am I right?' he enquired silkily. 'Because I know that I have, Suki.'

Suki felt tiny, cold beads of sweat break out on her forehead. She opened her mouth to speak, to deny the truth of what he'd said, but she was saved from the lie by Toby, who had obviously had enough of not being the centre of attention. He stared up at Pasquale pugnaciously. 'That Daddy's man!' he announced.

Suki tried very hard to imagine Pasquale as *anyone's* man, wondering if Toby's words might have offended his monumental ego, but she saw that he was laughing as he crouched down to Toby-height and smiled at the child.

'You're quite right,' he said gravely. 'How's your big wooden train set these days?'

'He go "choo"!' said Toby, delighted when Pasquale echoed 'choo-choo', in an astonishingly realistic impression of a steam-train. Surely there must be *something* he didn't excel at?

thought Suki. Yes, of course there was—tact and diplomacy!

'Where you going?' asked Toby.

'I heard your daddy say that you were going to the zoo, and I was kind of hoping that you might let me come with you. May I?'

'Yes!' grinned Toby.

Pasquale rose to his feet and Suki gave him a remonstrative look.

'That wasn't fair!' she protested.

He shrugged, then grinned, and the formidably handsome face became suddenly boyish. 'Who said anything about being fair? You know I'm dying to ride on a double-decker bus.' He gave her an outrageous little-boy look which nonetheless was devastatingly effective. 'You don't mind, do you, Suki?'

'And would it make any difference if I did?'

He shook his head as he took the folded push-chair from her and tucked it underneath his arm. 'Not a bit,' he replied cheerfully.

At the zoo, he took Toby on donkey rides and the old-fashioned carousel which was enjoying a revival. After each eating a burger for lunch they helped the keeper throw fish to the sea-lions and watched the big cats prowl around their reserve. And Pasquale teased Suki relentlessly when she refused to go into the reptile house with them. It came as a sudden shock to Suki to realise that she couldn't ever remember having quite so much fun.

She had never seen Pasquale look quite so re-laxed and she found herself staring at him curiously as Toby selected a particularly disgusting-looking ice-cream and Pasquale paid for it. 'I suppose you'll be telling me in a minute that you're prepared to change his nappy?' she asked frankly.

He gave her a half-smile, not the expected shudder which she had anticipated. 'I will if you want me to.'

'No,' she said hastily. 'It's OK.' And she began to study the wing colour of one of the parrots in the bird house as if her life depended on it.

But it wasn't so much his attitude towards *her* which was affecting her so much—it was his behaviour with Toby which was surreptitiously seeping into her defences and threatening them with imminent destruction. It was very difficult not to warm to a man who was so gentle with children.

She couldn't contain her curiosity any longer. 'You're very good with children,' she observed as she turned away from the parrot to face him, and then she blanched as a new and very disturbing thought tripped into her mind. 'You haven't got any of your own?' she asked before she had time to think about the question carefully.

He frowned. 'I'm not married,' he said immediately.

'So?'

The frown increased. 'So I'm an old-fashioned man at heart, Suki, and I would not contemplate having children out of wedlock.' He shook his head with a smile as he refused Toby's offer of a lick of ice-cream. 'Any knowledge I have, I have picked up from my niece. Francesca's daughter Claudia—she's a little older than Toby.'

'Francesca has a *daughter*?' exclaimed Suki.

He slanted her a look. 'What's so extraordinary about that?'

'Just that the other day you told me that she was a high-powered career-woman—'

'And the two are incompatible, is that it?' he cut in sardonically. 'As a matter of fact, in Francesca's case, they are. She has continued to work full-time, and Claudia has been brought up by a series of nannies, several of them entirely unsuitable, in my opinion.'

God, but he was autocratic! 'You sound as though you disapprove of working mothers,' she said, with deliberate understatement.

He nodded. 'I'm afraid that I do.'

'Afraid?' It seemed a curious choice of word.

The dark eyes glittered like chips of jet behind the dark, luxuriant lashes. 'I know it isn't the modern way of thinking, but I happen to believe that a child is best brought up predominantly by its parents—'

'But mainly the mother, of course?'

'That's right.'

If she was perfectly honest, she secretly agreed with him, but that was just her own emotional response, and intellectually Suki found herself leaping to the absent Francesca's defence. 'So a woman who may have spent many years establishing herself in a chosen career must then let

it all go because of the way that nature distri-
buted the hormones?'

He elevated his eyebrows into two dark, sardonic curves. 'I think that's oversimplifying
matters, don't you? A career can always be put
on hold—'

'Not one like mine,' put in Suki quickly, 'which
is age-dictated.'

His mouth twisted. 'No. Not one like yours.
But others can—'

'It's never quite the same,' said Suki stubbornly, 'as for a man.'

He stared at her very intently. 'No, of course
it isn't the same,' he agreed. 'But the hormonal
thing is a fact, and there's absolutely nothing we
can do to change that. Women have the babies;
men don't,' he finished.

'So in effect you're saying that equality between the sexes can't exist?' she challenged.

He wiped a blob of ice-cream which had fallen
from Toby's cone from one lean thigh and ab-
sently licked his finger. 'I prefer the concept of
compromise between the sexes, of acknowl-
edging the differences between them and working
around those differences.'

Suki plucked a tissue from her shoulder-bag
and bent down to wipe Toby's chin, before
straightening up. 'Is that why you've never
married?' she asked suddenly, wanting to know,
*needing* to know, and yet dreading to hear what
his answer would be. 'Because you've never
found anyone willing to agree to compromise

with what some people would say are your—er—rather outdated ideas about men and women?'

He stared fixedly into the distance, at a cluster of flamingoes which glowed golden and pink in the afternoon sunshine. 'You mean the conflict between career and maternal duty?' he asked. 'It's true that I tend to be attracted to the type of woman who *does* have a career, and, perversely, the type that would be least likely to give it up.

'But no, Suki.' And he turned to look at her, some indefinable spark lingering around the depths of his dark eyes. 'Quite apart from the fact that my own career is incompatible with family life, the reason that I have never married is that I've never met anyone I wanted to spend the rest of my life with.'

Suki bent down to unnecessarily wipe Toby's chin again, not wanting to look at Pasquale, painfully aware of the fact that she had been very subtly issued with a warning. Pasquale's analysis had, in effect, served to define the boundaries of any relationship which might occur between them. It was probably kinder that way, and sensible too. But his words hurt, and they only renewed her resolve not to get involved with him.

'It's getting late,' she said. 'We'd better be getting back.'

Unfortunately, not only did he treat Toby to piping-hot fish and chips on the way home, but he then insisted on accompanying her all the way back to Piers and Kirstie's house, and Kirstie smiled with delight when she saw him on the doorstep.

'I gatecrashed,' Pasquale explained, with a smile.

'Piers rang and said you were intending to. Do come in,' she urged, and to Suki's annoyance he agreed immediately.

He seemed to dominate the room with his dark, masculine presence, and Suki was left feeling like a small animal who had strayed unwittingly into a trap.

She spotted Toby tiredly rubbing his fists into his eyes and saw her escape route. 'Can I bath Toby for you?' she asked.

Kirstie's eyes crinkled at the corners. 'I'll give you three guesses!' she joked, and headed across the room towards the drinks cabinet.

Suki took far longer than was necessary. She and Toby splashed around with his rubber duck, before she washed his hair and brushed his teeth. She read him three Thomas the Tank Engine stories but once he was sound asleep there really was no excuse not to go back into the sitting room, so she reluctantly put the book back on his shelf. Surely Pasquale would have gone by now?

He hadn't.

He was sitting in one of the chintz armchairs sipping a glass of sherry and looking almost like part of the family.

Kirstie, who had been showing him some photos of Toby's christening, including an ap-palling one of Suki in a hat she had been persuaded to wear against her better judgement, looked up and smiled as she walked in the room.

'Is he OK?'

'Sound asleep. I washed his hair.'

'Did you?' asked Kirstie in admiration. 'How on earth did you manage that? He screams the place down when *I* do it! Sit down and have a sherry—you deserve one!'

Suki reluctantly refused to look into a pair of dark eyes which mocked her. 'I won't, thank you—'

'Nonsense!' said Kirstie. 'You certainly look as though you could do with one!'

They drank sherry and chatted about nothing in particular—or rather Kirstie and Pasquale did most of the talking, while Suki listened in moody silence as he turned on that careless charm, thinking that he really could have coaxed blood from a stone if he'd put his mind to it.

Even in the ordered calm of Kirstie's sitting room, drinking dry sherry in the early evening, she found it impossible not to be aware of his physical appeal—his almost overwhelming masculinity which lay coiled and tense beneath his outwardly cool and urbane appearance. Again and again, she had to resist the urge to let her eyes hungrily stray over towards him.

Eventually, she couldn't stand it any longer, and was just about to leave when Pasquale again surprised her, as he seemed to have been surprising her all day, by placing his empty glass down on a small table and getting to his feet. 'It's time I was going, Kirstie.' His eyes glittered as he looked down at Suki. 'May I offer you a lift anywhere?'

She shook her head. 'No, thank you. I'd planned to stay for a while.'

'Had you?' His tone was faintly mocking, but he didn't push it. 'Then don't linger too long, or you may be late for your date.'

Her *date*?

He gave her a sardonic smile as he read the genuine puzzlement in her eyes, and it took several seconds before the mists which had temporarily clouded her memory cleared. Of course! She'd lied about having a date this evening when he'd asked her to have dinner with him.

'You know, your date,' he reminded her coolly. 'Don't tell me you'd forgotten all about it, Suki?'

'N-no,' she stumbled. 'Of course not.'

Kirstie saw him to the door and when she came back into the sitting room she was still smiling. 'Oh, I *do* like that man!' she said. 'I've only met him once before,' she confided, 'but I thought he was absolutely *charming*.' She sighed. 'He took us for lunch to a beautiful restaurant overlooking Hyde Park—the three of us—Toby too. He made *such* a fuss of him, but then they say Italian men are very good with children. I know that he *is* Italian, but with that accent you can't really be sure, can you...?'

'No,' said Suki flatly, hoping that this was the end of the eulogy.

A questioning look grew in Kirstie's eyes, and Suki didn't think that she could face an interrogation—or rather she knew that wouldn't be able to lie to her sister-in-law.

'How are things?' she put in quickly, in her cheeriest manner. 'Generally.'

Kirstie shot her a look which spoke volumes. 'Generally? Fine. And specifically they're absolutely wonderful too. I could kiss that man Pasquale Caliandro. Since he took over the company, Piers is like a new man. Oh, he has the occasional moan—that's inevitable—but he works hard and he seems to have won his self-respect back. What's more, when he finishes work, he comes home—to *me*—not to some yuppy wine-bar!'

She blushed to the roots of her flaxen hair, and suddenly looked wildly young and pretty. 'We've been getting on better than we've done in a long, long time. And now that you've managed to change the subject,' she said perceptively, 'tell me one thing—*have* you got a date tonight?'

Suki shook her head. 'No.'

'Then why the hell didn't you let Pasquale give you a lift home?'

'Because I didn't want to.'

'Oh? And what's the matter with Signor Caliandro?'

'He's not my type.'

'Rubbish!' said Kirstie briskly. 'He's everybody's type! And it's quite obvious he's absolutely bananas about you!'

'No, he isn't,' said Suki gloomily. 'He just wants to go to bed with me.'

Kirstie giggled. 'Well, what's so wrong with that? That's what men generally *do* want to do, eventually, and I imagine that most women would be delighted to oblige.'

'That's just the trouble,' Suki said on a long sigh. 'I don't want to be "most women".'

Kirstie nodded and a look of comprehension slowly dawned in her bright blue eyes. 'Oh, I see,' she said slowly. 'We're talking exclusive here, are we, Suki? One-man one-woman stuff?'

That was exactly it. In one sentence, Kirstie had managed to hit on what Suki had been trying to deny that she wanted from Pasquale Caliandro since the moment she'd first met him. One-man one-woman stuff indeed. There was even a word for it.

Marriage.

Dumbly, she nodded.

'And how do you know that isn't what *he* wants?' persisted Kirstie.

Suki remembered his words at the zoo. About the kind of women he usually fell for. About never having met a woman he wanted to spend the rest of his life with. You couldn't get much clearer than that! 'He told me,' she said baldly.

Somehow she made her escape without breaking down and blubbing in front of Kirstie, but when she arrived back home she decided to indulge herself, and spent the remainder of the evening alternately calling him every name under the sun and trying not to burst into miserable tears. Because she had a make-up launch at the

Granchester tomorrow, and woe betide that her eyes should be swollen.

And, not for the first time lately, she finally fell asleep thinking how crazy it was to have a career which relied on something as unimportant as beauty.

## CHAPTER EIGHT

THE following morning, wearing blue shorts and a blue T-shirt with 'C'est Formidable!' emblazoned in gold across her bosom, Suki walked into the vast mirrored ballroom of the Granchester Hotel where the launch was taking place.

And Pasquale was the first person she saw—indeed the only person she saw.

Oh, there were loads of people milling around the place, but one darkly proud head registered itself in her field of vision as though she was destined to see only him.

Their eyes met; his were questioning and hers were—what? Oh, heavens, what were they? How much of herself did she give away with her eyes? Did he know that seeing him again had stirred her senses and her heart into life? Did he realise that when she saw Stacey Lomas bearing down on him she felt a primitive kind of jealousy overwhelming her like a tidal wave so that she felt like screaming out loud?

He nodded and smiled at something Stacey said to him, and then he walked over towards her. 'Hello, *bella*,' he said softly.

'Pasquale.' She inclined her head courteously.

'Did you sleep?' he enquired out of the blue.

'Of course I slept,' she lied. 'What on earth makes you think I didn't?'

'These.' And with his finger he touched the delicate skin beneath her eyes. 'There are faint blue smudges which even your make-up cannot disguise—'

'Oh, God!' Now even her looks were going to pieces. It was all very well moaning about her job, but if this continued she soon might not *have* a job! 'What about the photos?'

He shook his head. 'Don't worry. They'll be bleached out by the lights. I doubt whether anyone has noticed them. Except me,' he finished softly, and he sent her a lazy smile which was redolent of sheer, sensual promise.

Suki's skin prickled in helpless response. She felt dizzy just being *near* him, and knew that she had to get away from him quickly before she did something irrevocably stupid, like telling the man that she wanted him to marry her. 'Excuse me, Pasquale—I think they're ready to start shooting.'

'Wait.' He forestalled her with one hand placed on her arm. 'Have lunch with me afterwards.'

'No,' she said instantly.

'Why not?' he taunted softly. 'Afraid to?'

Not afraid—absolutely terrified. She opened her mouth to speak but he prevented her with a gentle shake of his head. 'Don't let's play these games any more, Suki,' he told her softly. 'I have a great deal that I need to say to you.' The dark eyes compelled her to look at him and it would have taken a stronger woman than Suki to resist that gaze.

The expression in his eyes was so mesmerising that she found it impossible to look away. 'What is it?' she whispered.

He shook his head. 'Not now. They're waiting for you. Let's have lunch. That's all.'

'Give me one good reason why, Pasquale,' she told him quietly.

'Because we both want to,' he said simply, and smiled. 'And, as I said, I need to talk to you. And what if I promised you that throughout the meal I would play the gentleman most assiduously?'

'Well, that I would *have* to see!' she mocked.

'Then so you shall. Come—Stacey's on her way over. Let's get these photographs done.'

It was past midday when they called a halt to the session, and Suki was beginning to regret ever having agreed to have lunch with him, but he swept aside all her protestations as he led her out of the ballroom and towards the lift.

'Where are we eating?' she enquired as he pressed the button.

'In my suite.'

For sheer effrontery, he was gold-medal class. She started to shake her head. 'If you think I'm going anywhere near your—'

But he stopped her with an emphatic, 'Suki?'

'What?'

'Didn't I give you my word? And if you stop to allow yourself to think about it instead of jumping to conclusions you'll agree that it's the ideal venue. Quite apart from the fact that it has one of the best views in London, I want privacy when I speak to you.' His eyes flicked over her outfit briefly. 'And I really don't imagine that you particularly want to go into a restaurant dressed like that.'

She had completely forgotten what she happened to be wearing, and looked down to see the gold Formidable logo which was emblazened all the way across her chest. Subtle it was *not*!

He sighed. 'But if you really cannot bring yourself to trust me, then we could go into the hotel boutique and get you kitted out in something more suitable before going down to the restaurant. Alternatively, we could take my car to your flat and I could wait while you get changed.' His eyes flicked to the gold watch which gleamed on his wrist. 'But if we do that you will miss your lunch, and you look as though you could do with some, because if I'm not mistaken you have lost weight in the last week.'

'Is it any wonder?' she retorted.

'No, not in the least,' he agreed quietly. 'You see, I too have had little appetite.' He saw the cynical look on her face. 'You don't believe me? Look—' And he laid one olive hand against the flat planes of his stomach, and Suki swallowed. Just about the last thing in the world she needed was an anatomy lesson, with Pasquale offering himself as a demonstrator!

'I'll take your word for it,' she said quickly.

It seemed that there was a separate lift just for Pasquale's suite, and when they had arrived at the eighteenth floor Suki could understand why.

They stepped straight out of it into a vast, white-carpeted area.

He saw her look of surprise as he gestured her towards one of the rooms off the main vestibule. 'It *is* rather spectacular, isn't it?' he said without boast as she followed him into the room he'd indicated, where a table was lavishly set. 'Do you see what I mean about the view?'

She did. It was breathtaking. 'It's—stunning,' she said faintly as she realised that she could actually read the numbers on Big Ben.

'Come through and I'll get you a drink,' he said.

She looked across at where the damask-covered table was laid with silver and cut glass. Tall candles stood waiting to be lit amidst a fragrant centrepiece of dark pink roses.

She stared at him, her amber eyes narrowing. 'This meal must have taken some foresight.'

He nodded. 'A little.'

'And were you really so certain that I would agree to have lunch with you?'

He didn't seem in the least perturbed by the accusation in her voice. 'I am not a betting man, Suki,' he smiled. 'I could not be certain—let's just say that I was pretty confident.'

'You are *so* arrogant,' she said quietly, and he laughed.

'I know,' he replied, unabashed. 'What are we going to do about it?'

'Absolutely nothing,' she said furiously. 'Because I've just changed my mind about lunch—'

'Suki,' he interrupted softly, 'I'm sorry if I've been flippant. Please stay.'

She willed her legs to move, but they stubbornly refused to obey her. Instead, with all the gullibility of a lamb being led to the slaughter, she allowed him to pull back a chair, and she sank down gratefully.

'Would you like some wine?' he asked her as he took his place opposite her.

She was half tempted to say no—lunchtime drinking always made her sleepy—but never in her life had she needed a drink so much and so she broke the habit of a lifetime. 'Yes, thank you,' she said.

He filled their glasses with the Chablis which was chilling in the ice-bucket beside him and Suki sipped at the fruity wine, appreciating the immediate feeling of relaxation which crept over her.

She put her glass down on the table and gave him a cool, quizzical look. 'So, Pasquale—what did you bring me here to talk about?' she asked, but he shook his head firmly.

'Not yet. First, eat,' he commanded.

She *hadn't* had much appetite recently, and she didn't think she could eat anything, but when she saw the giant peeled prawns, the delicate slivers of smoked salmon, and the delicious salads, she felt genuinely hungry for the first time in days.

All the time they ate, Pasquale talked to her about Franklin Motors, about the deal he'd just pulled off in New York, and even though she was fairly dense when it came to understanding finance he explained it so patiently, and in such simple terms, that she felt as though she could have walked out of the room and started dabbling successfully in the stock market!

She had just eaten her way through half a plateful of strawberries drenched in a raspberry coulis when she glanced up to find him silently watching her. The strawberries suddenly lost all their appeal, and she quickly put her spoon down.

'Let's take our coffee through to the drawing room,' he said. 'We can be more comfortable in there.'

Lulled by the good food and wine, Suki rose to her feet, and soon she was settled on one of the big, squashy white sofas, a demitasse of steaming coffee on the table in front of her, watching him pace the floor with the stealth and the grace of a tiger sizing up its prey.

Quite without warning, he suddenly said, 'I owe you an apology.'

It was the last thing in the world she had expected him to say. 'Oh?' she said, completely taken aback. 'For what?'

'For the way I have behaved towards you. Insulting you. Threatening you. And for not believing you when you spoke the truth.'

She wondered what particular truth he had in mind as she gazed at him in amazement. 'And what has brought about this sudden change of heart?'

'I spoke to Salvatore when I was in New York.'

'And?'

His mouth gave a wry twist. 'He convinced me that your relationship with him was purely professional. That you *were* simply mending his jeans.'

Suki held her breath for a moment. 'But *I* told you that!' she declared. 'And you didn't believe me!'

His mouth thinned into a hard line. 'I know. And I was wrong.'

'And that's it?' she queried incredulously. 'That's what the lunch and the view were in aid of—just to say that?'

'No, not just to say that,' he said, and shook his dark head. 'I have scarcely begun, *cara*.'

She leaned back against the sofa and gave him a steady stare. 'Oh?'

'How would you say that we got on yesterday?' he asked suddenly.

She blinked. 'Yesterday?'

'At the zoo,' he supplied, his dark eyes watching her very intently. 'Would you say that we got on well together, you and I?'

Suki looked at him in confusion.

'Be truthful,' he urged.

'Er, well . . .' She couldn't really *deny* it, could she? Not if she *was* being truthful. 'Yes,' she said eventually. 'Yes, I suppose we did.'

He grinned, and as always it made the hard lines of his face soften. 'Yes, we did. I thought so too. I enjoyed myself—more than I have enjoyed myself for a long time.'

'I'm not sure that I understand,' said Suki slowly, but the trouble was that she suspected that she understood what he meant only too well, and the disdain must have shown in her face. 'What point are you trying to make?'

'I just want you to ask yourself, Suki, who is benefiting from your refusing to acknowledge the attraction between us. Why do you continue to fight it? Fight me? Fight *us*?' he concluded huskily.

Her lips stayed open in genuine surprise. 'But there is no "us", Pasquale.'

'Isn't there? Tell me that you don't think of me every minute and I'll call you a liar,' he said, holding his hand up to silence her as she began to protest. 'There is no shame in admitting that,' he said. '*I* am admitting it, and for me it is something I am not used to—this obsession I have with you. Do you believe me when I tell you that?'

'Oh, yes—I *believe* you,' she answered coolly. 'It's because I haven't given in to you. You're a man who is used to getting everything he wants in life, whenever he wants it. Now you've found something that isn't just yours for the taking, and so you yearn for it all the more. If I went to bed with you this afternoon, you would have forgotten me by tomorrow.'

'*No!*' He shook his dark head in vehement denial. 'That is not so!' he contradicted softly. 'How can it be so when I have not forgotten you all these seven long years?'

Suki breathed out on a sigh as she shook her head, trying very hard not to read too much into his words.

'I still want you, Suki,' he said simply. 'More than I've ever wanted a woman before.'

'And am I supposed to thank you for making that astonishing declaration?'

He frowned, then shook his head. 'I'm not expecting your gratitude.'

'What, then? Just what are you expecting?'

He gave a restless shrug of his broad shoulders and as always when he tried to put his feelings into words his accent deepened and he became more Italian by the second. 'I've gone about this whole business badly, I know that. I have been impertinent, tactless even—saying that I wanted you to become my mistress. Even the word lover offended you. But how else can I say it, Suki? A relationship? How do your men usually put it?'

And with that last remark he damned himself. Her *men*! Good God, but it would amuse him to know that there hadn't been any! Not a single one! Wouldn't that feed his monumental ego even further?

She clasped her hands together so that he would not see that they were shaking with anger. Because for some reason the fact that he was dressing up his desire to bed her with this pseudo-respectable proposal of having 'a relationship' annoyed her far more than anything he had said to her before. At least when he had asked her to become his mistress he had been up front. What a hypocrite!

'"A relationship"?' she repeated faintly. 'I'm not sure exactly what you mean. Perhaps you could elaborate a little, Pasquale. How often would we see each other?'

She saw the gleam in his eyes as he anticipated victory. 'As often as our schedules allow. I'm away a lot, as you know, so our meetings will be somewhat erratic. Of course, now that you're under contract to me at Formidable it's going to be easier to *make* the time. Can you imagine how difficult it would have been if you'd still been jetting all over the place?'

How cold-blooded he sounded, she thought furiously, her blood boiling with rage. And then he smiled. He actually had the nerve to smile! What was more, it was the smooth, cruelly confident smile of a man secure in the knowledge that he'd got what he wanted.

*Her!*

'Tell me,' said Suki, choosing her words carefully, 'do you have girls in *all* the major cities?' She saw him frown, as if she'd puzzled him. 'Am I to be your girl in London?' she persisted coolly. 'And if that's the case, do I get exclusive access— or am I expected to share you? I suspect that Stacey might be rather put out.'

The anger on his face was so stark and menacing that she might have been intimidated under normal circumstances, but these *certainly* weren't normal circumstances.

'*What* did you say?' he asked, in a dangerously quiet voice.

But his anger was only matched by her own. She felt reckless with it, drunk with it. 'I wondered whether *Stacey* might mind,' she reiterated.

'Stacey?' He spoke the word as though it were foreign to him.

'Yes, Stacey! I don't know how broad-minded *you* might be, Pasquale, but I'm afraid that I really couldn't tolerate a threesome—'

'A *threesome*? Is that the kind of man you think I am?' he stormed, and if she had thought that she had seen him angry before that was nothing to the look of dark rage on his face now. 'A promiscuous man?'

'And is that the kind of woman you think I am?' she countered heatedly. 'The kind who could be cold-bloodedly propositioned like that? I'm surprised that you haven't had your damned lawyer draw up a contract with all your terms of agreement!' She got to her feet unsteadily. 'I'm sorry, but the answer is no. And now I think I'd better leave, before we say anything else we might regret.'

He was on his feet in an instant. All the anger had vanished from his face; she could read nothing in the implacable mask he now wore. 'Very well,' he said. 'I'll see you out.'

Perversely, stupidly, it hurt like hell that he was prepared to let her go so easily. He would never, she realised with a sinking heart, beg her to stay. He was far too proud a man to do that. 'Please don't bother—'

'I *said*,' he repeated, with soft menace, 'that I'll see you out.'

The silence which accompanied their walk into the main hall grew more awesomely oppressive by the second, and when he reached out to open the lift doors he turned to her, and his dark eyes pierced her with their intensity.

'Goodbye, Pasquale,' she said shakily, hating the finality of that tiny word, knowing instinctively that once she walked out of that door he would not pursue her again.

'Goodbye, Suki,' he said softly.

There was something so bitter-sweet and so unbearably poignant about the way he said it that for a moment Suki hesitated, torn with emotion, knowing that she must leave, and yet dreading the moment when she finally did.

And he was as motionless as she, as though he too wanted to prolong the moment, his gaze steady and intent while the air around them began to buzz with tension. She could see the pulse that was beating a rapid tattoo at his temple, and she found herself unable to tear her eyes away from him.

It was the softness in his face, and an imagined tenderness about his eyes, which was her undoing, and her own face softened in response. And when he commanded, in a quiet, low voice, 'Kiss me, Suki. Just once. Kiss me goodbye,' she couldn't have resisted him even if she'd wanted to.

Just one kiss, she told herself as wordlessly she went into his arms, and he drew her close, his embrace locking around her tightly as though he would never let her go.

*Dio mio,* he muttered in hoarse disbelief as he cupped her face between his hands to stare at her for a long moment, before lowering his head to take her mouth in a sweet, sweet kiss which she knew the moment it started could have only one possible conclusion. And when he raised his head at last there was a soft smile playing on his lips as he took in her dazed expression.

'That wasn't—fair,' she said shakily.

'What wasn't fair?'

'Kissing me.' She swallowed. 'Like that.'

'Like what? Like this?' And he bent his mouth to hers again, renewing the pressure and leaving her breathless and trembling in his arms. 'Like that?' he mocked gently.

'Yes,' she said helplessly.

'Who ever said anything about being fair?' he murmured into her hair as he held her tightly against him.

'But you promised,' she protested drowsily against his shoulder, aware of the slow, steady thudding of his heart which beat in unison with her own.

'I had my fingers crossed,' he told her shamelessly. 'And what price a promise if it means I stop fighting for what is worth fighting for?'

He stared down at her with a burning question in his eyes. 'Suki?' he asked unsteadily. 'If you don't want to, then just say so. I do not take what is not freely given.'

She knew what he wanted: her assurance that this was what she wanted, something indeed that she gave freely, not something he had coerced her into.

She shook her head. 'You know I want you, damn you,' she said in a trembling voice, and she read the raw exultation in his eyes as he brought his mouth down onto hers. And if there had been any lingering doubt in her mind it was banished with that kiss.

He wasn't at all how she'd thought he would be. She had imagined urgency in his embraces, an impassioned but brief coupling as he sought to douse the fires of his desire which had been raging in his blood for so long.

But it was not a bit like that.

Even with her inexperience, she sensed his restraint as he continued to kiss her, as though he couldn't get enough of her lips, as though he were drowning in their sweetness. And his obvious approbation gave her the courage to cast her inexperience aside, to stop *thinking* and to allow her heart to govern the movements which she found were purely instinctive.

Her hands crept to the broad, muscular bank of his shoulders, curving possessively around his neck, and then she allowed her fingers to roam in glorious abandon in the rich lushness of his hair.

He made a small sound of assertion as he brought her even closer into his body, so that they fitted as perfectly as a hand inside a glove, and she was made achingly aware of the hard throb of his desire which pushed insistently against her.

His mouth was now kissing the soft skin at her neck, and her head was tipped back to allow him access to as much of her flesh as possible. She felt him pulling the T-shirt away from the waistband of her shorts, felt his hand skating slowly beneath towards her acutely aroused breasts, tantalising and tormenting her by refusing to caress them.

She gave a helpless little whimper as she felt his fingers brush lightly over the silk of her bra, then capture one nipple and play with it almost idly, until she felt her knees begin to give way.

He drew his mouth away from hers, and she shuddered at how bereft that abandonment made her feel.

'Now,' he asserted, in a harsh kind of voice.

'Yes, now,' she affirmed shakily. 'Yes, Pasquale, *yes* . . . now.'

Without another word he swept her up into his arms and carried her through to the bedroom, where he laid her on top of the vast bed. The curtains were drawn and the room was dim as he peeled off her T-shirt and let it flutter to the floor.

His eyes were blazing as he gazed at her breasts almost dazedly. 'Oh, *cara*,' he murmured before he bent his head to sweetly suckle one nipple, the silk of the bra growing wet and clingy beneath his mouth.

Suki was lost in a world of feeling. Hot, erotic sensations sprang into life in her body. Her breasts were heavy and swollen as he freed them from the restraint of the flimsy little bra she wore and explored their generous curves with enticing movements of his hands and mouth.

He slid the shorts off, then pulled his own T-shirt over his head, his eyes never leaving her face as he unbuckled his belt and unzipped his jeans. And when she saw the magnificent power of him springing free as he removed his briefs she felt like a delicious voyeur and she slowly ran her tongue over her bottom lip, deliberately provocative, saying nothing, promising everything.

He was naked when he came to lie beside her, studying her face intently as he stroked each breast in turn, watching her reaction as his hand moved slowly all the way up the slender length of her leg, pausing to stroke enticing little circles at the soft skin of her inner thigh, which had her moving around in restless frustration, until he took pity on her and his finger moved inside her panties, finding her moist and hot and wanting, wanting, wanting...

'Tell me what it is you like, what it is you want,' he whispered against her mouth as she moved her hips restively. 'I'll give you anything, *cara*, anything you want. Just tell me.'

She scarcely heard his words, she was so caught up in the magical movement of his hands and his lips against her skin. 'Just you,' she said huskily. 'Only you.'

He seemed to lose something of his restraint then, skimming the panties off with a breathless haste it thrilled her to witness, and it didn't even embarrass her when he took a small packet from the locker and began to undo it. She watched as he protected himself—and her—from any repercussions of their lovemaking, and was unable to repress the distinct and totally illogical pang of disappointment which his action produced.

But she forgot everything as he came to lie on top of her, his mouth whispering something incomprehensible into her ear as he entered her with one fierce thrust.

He suddenly stilled as he felt her stiffen from the brief pain which pierced her, her fingernails automatically digging into his back, and she felt the muscles beneath tense up.

*'Madre di Dio!'* he husked in a strangely gritty tone.

Had he guessed? she wondered. Of course he had guessed—but what now? Men as experienced as Pasquale probably wouldn't welcome a virgin in their beds. So what—*what* if he stopped?

Oh, he couldn't.

He couldn't.

The pain a distant memory, Suki began to move her hips, guided by some infinitely welcome instinct, so that on a shuddering sigh he began to move again, more slowly now, and then deeper—deeper and fiercer, each powerful thrust taking her closer and closer to something so exquisite, so unbearably exquisite that she was afraid to acknowledge it for fear that it might prove to be some impossible dream.

And when it did happen it took her completely by surprise. She gave a strangled little noise of disbelief as it began, his name wrenched from her lips on a sob as the first heavenly wave of bliss came, then another, and another—the contractions gradually becoming ripples which stilled into a lethargy that begged for sleep. And Pasquale tensed on one last frantic movement as he climaxed, a small cry escaping his lips as he buried his face in her hair.

They lay tangled together for what could have been seconds or minutes or even hours. Suki felt the beat of her heart gradually slowing to normal. Her head resting against his neck, she was feeling as warm and indolent as a cat stretched before a fire, and yet her thoughts lay in confusion because the situation was completely outside her experience. She had no idea what Pasquale would say or do next. Would he be mockingly triumphant that she had done just what she had vowed not to?

But he surprised her—as he always seemed to be surprising her. He propped himself up on one elbow, a look bordering on regret shading his dark eyes.

'So, Suki,' he said, softly, 'you let me find out in the very worst way possible that you were a virgin...'

The very *worst* way? How horribly censorious he made that sound. Biting her lip, Suki turned her face away from him, but with a gentle hand he moved her back towards him.

'Don't you know that I could have hurt you?' he whispered. 'Hell, Suki, I *did* hurt you, didn't I?'

'Not really. Only a little.'

'I would have been so much more gentle with you had I known.'

'Why? Do your virgins usually announce the fact to you proudly?' she fired back, and closed her eyes before she did something as stupid as crying.

He said something soft and profound beneath his breath, but still she kept her eyes tightly shut. 'Suki?'

'What?'

'Open your eyes and look at me.'

'No.'

'*Yes.*'

Reluctantly, she did as he asked, her chin rising defiantly. 'Why?'

He smiled, the most lazy, relaxed smile she had ever seen him give, and it melted her resolve immediately. 'Would you like me to show you what it can be like when it doesn't hurt at all?'

And, with his naked flesh pressing against hers, his mouth against her neck and his fingers brushing lightly from breast to thigh, there was only one thing she could possibly say. 'You know I would,' she answered, her voice shaky, her body greedily anticipating what was to come, while her mind mocked her. Because, despite all her good intentions, it had been as easy as breathing to end up in Pasquale's bed ...

So this is what being a mistress is all about, thought Suki as she sat wearing a bra and a pair of French knickers in Pasquale's bedroom one morning, staring at herself in the mirror. From the bathroom came the sound of the shower running and Pasquale was singing something softly in Italian. He sounded happy, but of course he was happy. He was always happy after they'd made love. Which made him happy ninety per cent of the time, she thought waspishly.

Not that she was really complaining about *that* particular aspect of the relationship. They kept *meaning* to go to the theatre, for a drive out into the country, but they never seemed to make it beyond the bedroom. And she adored making love just as he did. It was just...just...

Suki began to brush her hair, unable to rid herself of the niggly feeling of dissatisfaction.

Yet surely she had everything she wanted? Pasquale was kind, attentive, witty, funny. He made the most beautiful love imaginable. So *why* was it not enough?

The answer was simple: because he hadn't said one word to her that didn't indicate that she was anything more than the latest in a long line of lovers, and she couldn't help the insecurity which made her wonder when she was likely to be replaced. And consequently, instead of flowering and blossoming within the relationship, she sometimes found herself displaying a remoteness which she used as a shield to protect herself against future hurt.

After their first night together, he had asked her to move in with him, a request he had since repeated daily, but on this she had been adamant.

'No, Pasquale,' she had answered coolly, and had seen the dangerous glitter in his dark eyes.

'But why not?' he had demanded.

'Because I value my independence!' she'd lied, knowing that the real reason was that the less she gave, the less she would be hurt.

'You drive me mad! Crazy! Do you know that, Suki?' he'd exploded, in what was these days a

rare display of temper, his accent deep and pro-
nounced. 'The first woman I've ever asked to
move in with me, and you say no!'

'Well, you know what they say,' she'd answered
elusively. 'That the grass is always greener on the
other side!' And she had drifted off into the
bathroom, hearing his low growl of rage.

'Why are you pulling such an angry face?'
came a low voice, and Pasquale's reflection
loomed behind her in the mirror, his hands
dropping to her shoulders. 'And why do you sit
around in nothing but your underwear?' he murmured on a kind of groan. 'So that I want to take
you back to bed and—'

He looked swiftly down at his watch and shook
his head impatiently. 'There isn't time. I have this
wretched meeting to attend.' He dropped a soft
kiss onto one bare shoulder, and Suki's heart
clenched as she covertly watched the dark head.
Oh, how she loved the wretched man! No matter
what she told herself, nothing could change that.

'There's always later,' she murmured, tipping
her head back so that he could kiss her mouth.

'I'll be home at one,' he said huskily. 'Will you
be here?'

'I might.'

'Promise me, *cara*.'

'I'll be here,' she said, smiling, unable to resist
him.

'I'll take you out for lunch.'

'That'd be nice.'

He kissed her goodbye and she went back to
her flat and changed. Answered a few bills. There

was no Formidable job until Saturday and yet she wished that she had something to occupy her mind. She sometimes felt as though she was standing in the wings watching a play of her own life, only taking central stage whenever Pasquale was around.

She arrived back at his suite at five to one, wearing one of his favourite outfits—a simple white button-through sundress—with nothing but a pair of white lacy panties underneath.

She picked up a book and, curling her feet up beneath her, settled down to read it while she waited for him.

And waited.

And waited.

At two-thirty he still wasn't there, and so Suki rang down for a sandwich, then left most of it untouched.

She began to worry. What if he'd had an accident? She didn't even know where he'd gone, for heaven's sake—other than he was out on business—and that could mean almost anything.

She was a jittery mixture of anxiety and anger by ten to four, when the phone rang. She snatched it up as if it were a lifeline.

'Pasquale?' she said.

There was a pause, and then a female voice said, 'Miss Franklin?'

'Yes.'

'Pasquale—Signor Caliandro—asked me to call you to tell you that regretfully he is being held up longer than he anticipated.'

'May I speak to him, please?' asked Suki.

'I'd rather not disturb him,' came the cool reply.

'I see.' Did the woman sound mildly amused, or was that simply Suki's paranoia? She took a deep breath. 'Thank you so much for informing me.'

'My pleasure.' There was a click as the line was disconnected.

Suki almost threw the phone down and began to pace up and down the vast sitting room with its amazing views over the Thames.

How dare he? she thought furiously. How *dare* he keep her waiting then have some female, some *minion*—or *was* she?—telephone her almost three hours later to tell her that he would be late? What kind of person did he think she was that he could treat her in such a way?

Suki was brought up short. A mistress, that was who. That was how men treated women who had no place in their lives bar in the bedroom. Oh, yes, they gave them great sex—but zilch in the way of respect.

She could never remember having been so angry in her whole life; she was literally shaking with rage. Then her gaze came to rest on Pasquale's wallet lying on the coffee-table and inspiration came to her in a flash. Well, if he wanted to treat her like a mistress, then she'd jolly well *behave* like one!

Unrepentantly, she skimmed through it until she found what she was looking for, and then she slammed her way out of the suite and downstairs to order herself a cab.

*     *     *

She arrived back at six, struggling under the weight of all the carrier bags she'd accumulated. She took them straight into the master bedroom, stopping short when she saw that Pasquale was lying on the bed, wearing nothing but a pair of jeans, surveying her from between narrowed eyes.

'Well, hello,' he said, in a tone she couldn't quite decipher. 'I was wondering where you'd got to.'

Suki dropped the carrier bags on the floor and looked down at him, her mouth compressed into an angry line. '*Were* you?'

'Naturally,' he said blandly, but his eyes were very watchful. 'Where have you been?'

'What right do you have to ask me where I've been, when you never bother to tell me where *you're* going?'

'That's because you never ask me. In fact you show no interest whatsoever in what I'm doing, do you, Suki?'

'Because I'm your *mistress*!' she yelled. 'And mistresses *have* no rights, do they? Outside the bedroom, of course.'

A nerve began to flicker dangerously in his cheek. 'Are you going to tell me where you've been?'

'Yes, I'll tell you! I've been out...' She paused deliberately as she let his credit cards flutter in a plastic clatter onto the coffee-table. '*Buying,*' she emphasised.

'That's nice,' he said, in a voice devoid of any emotion. 'Buying what?'

Suki shrugged. 'Whatever took my fancy. I spent hundreds of pounds and I used your credit cards. I do hope you don't mind—but that's what mistresses do, isn't it, Pasquale—go out and run up huge bills?'

She saw a spark of something raw and frightening in his eyes but when he spoke he sounded horribly calm. 'You think I treat you like a mistress, do you, Suki? Oh, no,' he said softly, shaking his head. 'But if you like I can demonstrate to you how a mistress really *should* be treated.' His eyes flickered over her body. 'Show me what you've bought,' he commanded in a velvety voice.

Suki swallowed. There was something in his eyes which vanquished all her anger, something in his voice which started an aching deep within her.

She shook her head, aware that she'd gone just that bit too far. 'I can settle up with you—'

'Show me,' he repeated softly.

Her heart pounding, she bent to the carrier bag and lifted out the first thing which came to hand—a short black dress in clinging Lycra.

'Put it on,' he said harshly.

'Pasquale—I didn't mean—'

'Put it on,' he interrupted brutally. 'Now.'

She stared into his hot, dark eyes and with faltering fingers she began to undo the buttons of her white sundress, then noticed that he was unbuckling the belt of his trousers...

'Pasquale!' she cried out in excited alarm.

'Take the dress off,' he said softly, and he continued to undress.

Trembling with hunger, she did as he asked, until she stood before him wearing nothing but her briefs, and she blushed as he kicked his jeans off and she saw just how aroused he was. Quickly, she lifted up the black dress to put it on.

'*No!*' His eyes glittered, and there was a long, tense pause. 'Take off your panties,' he said deliberately.

'Pasquale...'

'Take them off,' he repeated.

She slid them down her thighs, so unbearably excited that she could hardly step out of them, so relieved, so exquisitely relieved when he reached out to pull her down onto the bed. He covered her body with his own and thrust into her without warning. It should have been shameful, humiliating—but it was the most exciting thing that had ever happened to her and, crying out, she couldn't prevent herself from convulsing helplessly around him and almost immediately she felt him shudder within the circle of her arms.

Afterwards there was complete silence in the room, save the sound of laboured breathing gradually returning to normal, and then Pasquale suddenly withdrew from her and rolled over onto his back.

He lay motionless, staring in silence at the ceiling, his face as forbidding as stone, his body tensed as if for a fight. It was as if she wasn't even in the room with him, let alone lying on the bed next to him.

And once the fire had died down in her blood Suki felt completely and utterly empty. *She* had become his mistress. He had not forced her; she had only herself to blame. And *she* had provoked him into that frantic, loveless coupling just now. What else would they provoke each other into before it was all over?

It was in that instant that Suki knew that she needed to get out of his life before she destroyed herself and her self-respect. She drew in a silent breath to prepare herself for a retreat with as much dignity as possible, knowing that she could not possibly get dressed while he lay awake. What if he tried to persuade her to stay? Used that formidable charm and power and sexual potency to make her change her mind?

No, she silently vowed. She didn't want words or awkwardness; she wanted *out*. Of his suite and his arms and his life. With a little sigh, she snuggled into the pillow, her breathing becoming slow and steady as she affected sleep.

She didn't know how long it took for Pasquale to fall asleep beside her. She could tell from the rustle of the sheets that twice he turned to face her, but he spoke not a word and she maintained her charade of serene sleep brilliantly.

It seemed like an eternity, but was probably only ten or fifteen minutes, before eventually she was rewarded with the sound of his slow, steady breathing, and she expelled a soft sigh of relief. She didn't dare risk getting dressed in the bedroom for fear of waking him, so she crept around like a thief, locating her clothes, which she literally threw on in the hall.

The lift was, thankfully, empty, and she raked a brush through her tousled hair and tried to wipe the smudges of mascara from beneath her eyes. But her appearance told the story of a woman who had just been thoroughly ravished, and it took every bit of pride she had to meet the knowing, rather amused stare of the man behind the reception desk.

'May I help you, miss?' he asked.

'You may,' she answered with dignity. 'I'd like some hotel notepaper and an envelope, please. Oh, and a pen.'

'Certainly,' he answered, and placed them on the desk in front of her.

She kept the note short and to the point. It said, 'You paid $5,000,000 for it; I hope it was worth it. Suki.' She placed it in the envelope, sealed it, and handed it to the receptionist.

'Please see that Signor Caliandro gets this, would you?'

'Yes, miss.'

And as she swung out of the hotel she realised that today, for the first time, Pasquale hadn't bothered to use any contraception...

# CHAPTER NINE

THE old-fashioned doorbell clanged alarmingly and Suki screwed her nose up, tempted to ignore it, but it clanged again, and more insistently this time.

'I'm coming!' she yelled, and dipped her paintbrush into the jar of linseed, her eyes going ruefully to the large canvas she had been working on for the last fortnight.

Admit it, she thought. It's rubbish. Total and absolute rubbish. You've changed your whole life around so that you can pursue some crazy dream of painting, and now you discover that you can't.

And she knew why.

Didn't legend have it that a broken heart was supposed to inspire creative activity?

But not, it seemed, in her case. In her case it had simply deadened it.

The doorbell rang a third time.

'OK!' She pulled the door open and stared into dark and formidable eyes of jet, and for a moment she really thought that she might be about to faint.

'P-Pasquale...' she said tremulously, her defences immediately weakened by the shock of seeing him in the glorious, vital flesh. She took a deep breath. 'I don't want to see you,' she said tightly.

'Yes. You've made that fairly obvious,' he replied.

'*Pasquale!*' she exclaimed as he strode unasked over the threshold. 'Wh-what do you think you're doing?'

'I'm coming in. What does it look like?'

'You can't do that!'

'I just have,' he returned grimly. He turned to face her, his eyes skimming over her, taking in her pale, pinched face, the auburn hair worn in a functional french plait.

And she stared back at him, feasting her eyes on the man she had ineffectually forbidden herself to think about. The dark hair was ruffled, his chin slightly more shadowed than usual. The elegant silk tie was knotted casually, without its accustomed care. He looked like a man who had dressed in a hurry, and it made the bile rise in her throat as her jealous mind immediately leapt to one very painful conclusion as to why that might be.

'If you've come threatening litigation because I've broken my contract—' she began.

'No, Suki,' he interrupted coolly. 'That isn't why I'm here.'

Suki swallowed. Having over six feet of dark and brooding-looking male in the sitting room of the tiny country cottage she was renting made it look like a Wendy house. 'How the hell did you find me?' she demanded.

'It wasn't easy,' he admitted grimly, 'when you left town without a word, and so quickly. You made your disappearance fairly conclusive, Suki.'

'That's what I intended to do,' she returned coolly.

'Obviously.'

'So how did you find me?'

'Your agent told me. Eventually.'

'Carly told you? Why on earth should she do that, when I gave her strict instructions not to—?'

'I appealed to her better judgement.'

'You had no right to do that!'

'Wrong, Suki—I had every right, including the right which demands to know whether you are carrying my child.'

Suki's heart began to beat wildly in her chest. 'Pasquale, I—'

'Are you, Suki?' he demanded suddenly. 'Carrying my child?'

The world seemed to spin on its axis.

'Are—you—pregnant?' he said. 'Because I need to know.'

'No,' she answered quietly, swallowing back the sudden salty taste in her mouth. She had found out a week after she had left his hotel room and the discovery hadn't given her the relief she had expected to feel. Instead, she had spent the whole day crying, feeling that she had been robbed of something incredibly precious.

He let out a small sigh and Suki was appalled at how profoundly his obvious relief wounded her. Just what would he have done if she *had* been pregnant? she wondered angrily. 'Why do you want to know?' she asked.

His eyes narrowed as if her question had surprised him. 'Why?' he repeated mockingly, and Suki felt all her suppressed rage and grief and hurt begin to bubble up inside her.

'Yes, why? Do you normally have to follow your bed-partners up to find out whether you're going to be a daddy or not?'

He stared at her assessingly. '*Normally*,' he answered coolly, 'they don't run quite so swiftly from my bed.'

'I'll bet they don't!' she declared wildly, her face flaring with a hot, jealous flood of blood. 'Well, don't worry, Pasquale—this time you were lucky—'

'Lucky?' he interjected, that speculative look replaced by one of barely contained anger, and his voice sounded suddenly harsh with incredulity. 'Luck was not on my side when I failed to impregnate you. As was my intention,' he added deliberately, his eyes flashing a darkly arrogant challenge at her.

'Your—intention?' she repeated weakly.

His eyes narrowed. 'Naturally. I have never had unprotected sex with a woman. Except with you, Suki. And, believe me, it was no accident. It was a deliberate oversight. Although in the circumstances it was an easy oversight to make—you'd got me so hot for you that I could barely think straight.'

Disbelief warred with some deep, primitive longing as she struggled to make sense of his words. 'You mean—' the words stumbled out

'—that you were actually *trying* to get me pregnant?'

'I was making love to you,' he corrected her. 'But if in the process I made you pregnant, then yes, I would have been an extremely happy man.'

Her head was spinning. 'But why on earth should you want to do that?' she asked in bewilderment.

He studied her for a long moment, before nodding, as though he had come to a decision. 'I am not proud of my behaviour towards you, Suki. Without thought, I have robbed you of your virtue. I have falsely accused you of many things, and for that I am bitterly ashamed.'

Which didn't answer her question at all. 'But I still don't understand why you wanted to get me pregnant,' she said slowly.

He threw her an odd look. 'Don't you? Don't you really? Why does a man suddenly find that he wants to spend every moment, both waking and sleeping, with one woman? Why does a man want this certain woman, and only this one woman, to bear his children? It's called love, Suki.' His voice was very soft. 'And what does that man do when the woman he loves has made it clear to him that she does not feel the same way? I wanted you so badly that I was prepared to tie you to me in the most basic way there is—through procreation.'

She opened her mouth in disbelief, but no words came. He had just said that he loved her, and the words meant nothing. 'You're lying,

Pasquale!' she accused shakily. 'You're lying to me!'

He shook his head. 'It's no lie, Suki. Don't you know that I love you? As I think I have probably loved you since you first came to my house as a teenager, standing in the sunshine with that mane of hair all fiery and magnificent and blazing. And the way you used to let your head droop and then slant those golden eyes at me made me have all kinds of wicked desires that kept me awake at night.'

He shook his head. 'But I didn't dare admit what I was feeling and so I fought it. Every damned step of the way. I was trying so desperately to look on you as the schoolfriend of my little sister, and feeling as guilty as hell because the more I saw you, the more I wanted you. It was far easier to learn to hate you after that night of the storm than to admit to the frightening alternative: that I was in love with you.'

It was lies, all lies, and Suki forced herself to quell the wild hope that his words inspired. 'But you threw me out,' she pointed out. 'Remember? Insulted me and treated me with the utmost disdain.'

'And don't you know *why*?' he demanded. 'You were still at school! You were only seventeen, for heaven's sake. I was older, experienced—you were a mere child—a guest in my house, and as such I was responsible for you— *morally* responsible and *physically* responsible. I had no right to abuse my position and power. I very nearly lost control that night—*I*—' he shook his head '—who had never lost control in my life. And I fooled myself, Suki,' he said savagely. 'In so many, many ways.'

'Fooled yourself?' she said, not understanding. 'How?'

'By allowing myself to pretend that I had not known that I was making love to you, that I was half-asleep and that I believed it was someone else. By allowing myself to believe that you were morally corrupt and a bad influence on my sister.

'It took me quite a while to admit that in my heart I had suspected all along that Francesca had been running wild at school since the death of our mother. My father made a mistake in sending her away to Switzerland—a mistake which I had sanctioned in allowing her to go there, since Father was too interested in his beautiful young wife to care much about Francesca's welfare.'

He shook his head, his expression pained. 'It made it easier for me to believe that her behaviour was due to *your* influence. I did that because it was the only way I could cope with the knowledge that I had almost made love to a girl of such tender years. And the only way I could prevent myself from taking you, over and over again, was to convince myself that I despised you. Because no matter how much I wanted you you were too young, Suki. Much, much too young.'

He paused, and the dark, beautiful eyes glittered like jet. 'But I never forgot you, nor stopped wanting you. And when I read about your supposed liaisons with other men it only served to reinforce my prejudice that you were a beautiful but faithless woman—'

'Someone like your stepmother?' she cut in shrewdly, suddenly understanding the influence of the role model that *he* had grown up with, and he nodded slowly.

'I'm afraid that I was guilty of the age-old mistake of dividing women into two categories and judging them.'

'And I certainly wasn't in the Madonna category?' guessed Suki drily.

He shook his head. 'Correct. I had started making plans to bring you back into my life, when my secretary told me that you'd secretly gone off for the weekend with her fiancé, who, incidentally, used to idolise you—'

Her head began to spin and Suki frowned, not understanding. 'You mean—you mean you'd started buying Formidable *before* you saw me in the South of France?'

He smiled. 'But naturally. Did you think otherwise?'

'Of course I did!'

He shook his head. '*Cara*, contrary to what the storybooks tell you, one cannot take over a corporation the size of Formidable overnight—it takes months of planning. As I said, I was eaten up with jealousy at the thought of you cavorting with Salvatore, and yet I was rejoicing in this early opportunity to see you again before I offered you the Formidable contract.

'And when I *did* see you I realised that I was still as vulnerable to your spell. And still I tried to resist. I tried to tell myself you were everything I despised in a woman. And at times I even convinced myself that I hated you. But at others . . .' His voice trailed off and he looked at her with intent, dark eyes.

'So you invested in Franklin Motors because—'

'Because I needed to have something to fall back on if you refused to accept the Formidable contract, which was not inconceivable.'

'You ruthless swine,' remonstrated Suki, but only half-heartedly. He had bought a company and invested in another because he loved her. She shivered in delight.

'But what I still don't understand,' he queried softly, and his eyes were full of genuine puzzlement, 'is that if I, as I now know I was, was your first and only lover, then why on earth didn't you sue all those damned newspapers for the lies they printed about you?'

Suki shrugged her narrow shoulders. 'I was persuaded not to—it would have been too much hassle, for one thing. Plus I had no desire to have some ambitious counsel try to pull me to pieces on the witness stand.'

He shook his head distractedly. 'I should have guessed, Suki. I should have *known* that there was something so fundamentally sweet and sound at the very core of you. You had far too much pride and dignity ever to have been promiscuous. One by one you gradually blew away my preconceptions, until all that remained was the certain knowledge of how deeply I cared for you.'

'But why didn't you just *tell* me all this?' she demanded. 'Why didn't you tell me that you loved me, instead of all this business about me becoming your mistress?'

He shrugged. 'Pride, for one thing. Because I was convinced that such a volte-face would be implausible after everything I had said and done. And because I was not sure how forgiving—if at all—your nature would be, especially where I was concerned. I was completely in the dark about your feelings for *me*, and that is why I thought it advisable to take things one step at a time.

'I thought that if I gave you time your feelings of anger towards me might one day change into something else. But it didn't work out like that. Instead of growing closer, we seemed to be growing more distant—'

'Because I *hated* being thought of as your mistress. It made me feel expendable—'

'Then why the hell didn't you tell me?'

'Pride too, I suppose—and I hoped that I wouldn't have to—that you might guess. Pasquale,' she said half-exasperatedly, 'didn't you even stop to think about why I had given you my—virtue?' She hesitated as she used his own word. An old-fashioned word. She liked it.

He lifted his hands in supplication. 'I was so crazy about you that I didn't stop to analyse it until after you'd gone, and when I did I realised that you would not have given me something so precious unless you cared about me...' His voice tailed off as his eyes asked a question.

She lifted a hand and laid it very gently on his cheek. 'I wish I *was* carrying your child,' she said softly. 'I wish it more than anything in the world.'

'Suki?'

She smiled at him. 'Yes, I love you. I've always loved you, you idiotic man—don't you know that? Pasquale—'

But she never got to finish what she'd been saying, because suddenly she was in the place she most wanted to be: in Pasquale's arms.

And he was kissing her as if he'd just discovered kissing and it was several breathless minutes before he lifted his head to stare down at her gravely.

'Those things I said about working women giving up their careers to look after children . . .'

'Mmm?' she asked dreamily.

'Forget them.'

'*Forget* them? That's very magnanimous of you, Pasquale,' she declared, her amber eyes sparking with mischief.

'I can't possibly dictate terms like that. I love you and I want you to be happy.'

'Enough to compromise your theories on child-rearing?'

The broad shoulders were lifted in the smallest of shrugs. 'Oh, yes, my darling. You are a successful woman, and your career is very important to you. I know that. I couldn't possibly ask you to give up everything you've worked for.'

She decided to put him out of his misery. 'Oh, yes, you could!'

'Hmm?' He bent his head to kiss the soft skin of her neck, then paused and lifted it up to stare at her. '*What* did you say?'

'That I agree with you,' she said complacently, amused by the perplexed look which appeared in his dark eyes. 'I think mothers should be with their children, if that's what they want to do. And I do.'

'That's not what you implied the other day,' he said drily. 'The other day you tried to tear my argument to pieces.'

'That's because the other day we were talking hypothetically,' she said firmly. 'And I was standing up for Francesca. Call it sisterhood, if you like. Seriously, Pasquale—I've been growing disenchanted with modelling for some time now. And you always told me that I ought to paint— well, that's what I'm going to do, and painting will fit in very well with family life. In fact, that's what I've been doing since I came to live here.'

For the first time in several minutes his eyes left her, and fell on the canvas she'd been working on when he'd arrived, and a shrewdly assessing look came into his eyes as he studied it.

'What do you think?' she asked suddenly.

'It—' He hesitated and winced very slightly. 'It isn't one of your—better pictures, *bella mia*.'

She gave a sigh of relief. He loved her! He loved her enough to tell her the truth! 'I know it isn't. In fact it's rubbish. My heart hasn't been in it because I've been so miserable—'

'And why have you been miserable, *cara*?' he asked innocently as he began to unbutton her shirt.

'You know very well why.' And she leaned back to make the unbuttoning easier.

'Tell me anyway?' he suggested as the shirt fluttered to the floor. 'Better still, why not show me? And afterwards we can discuss our wedding.'

'Our wedding? I can't remember you asking to marry me.'

'Easily remedied,' he murmured as he carried her off into the bedroom. 'Will you marry me, my beautiful golden-eyed girl?'

'You know I will, you arrogant brute!'

'But soon, *cara*. It must be soon,' he told her sternly. 'I am not prepared to wait for something that means so much to me. As I told you once before, I'm not a—'

'*Patient man!*' she finished, laughing up at him. 'And I am not a very patient woman, so will you please make love to me right now, Pasquale?'

He smiled down at her lovely face as he lay down beside her on the bed. '*Amore mio,*' he murmured softly, shaking his dark head in bemused wonderment, and he bent down and slowly began to kiss her.

# HARLEQUIN PRESENTS®

**They say it's the quiet ones
you have to watch...**

Isobel a temptress?
Patrick couldn't believe it—she seemed
so modest, so reserved.

But then he, too, began to fall under her spell...

Find out more in Anne Mather's new story
**#1869 WICKED CAPRICE**

Available in March wherever
Harlequin books are sold.

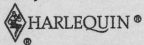

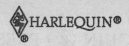 **HARLEQUIN®**

## *Not The Same Old Story!*

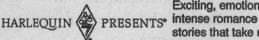

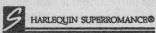